Too Hot to Ride

Praise for Andrews & Austin

Combust the Sun

"In a succinct film-style narrative, with scenes that move, a character-driven plot, and crisp dialogue worthy of a screenplay, Andrews & Austin have successfully crafted an engaging Hollywood mystery."—*Just About Write*

Summer Winds

"Andrews & Austin never, never disappoint their fans. Their wit and intelligence sing from the pages."—*Just About Write*

Uncross My Heart

"The one-liners come fast and furiously, but it's the relationship between two bright, intelligent women that resonates long after the last page has been turned."—*Ellen Hart, Lambda Literary Award–winning author of the Jane Lawless Mystery series*

"Andrews & Austin weave religion and romance together in a story that tackles a serious issue with bracing humor, and that balances provocative thought with sensual entertainment."
—*Richard Labonte, Q-Syndicate*

Mistress of the Runes

"With its humorous depiction of glamorous careers and corporate shenanigans, in *Mistress of the Runes*, Andrews & Austin once again offer readers sheer entertainment. They manage to playfully sustain a teasing erotic tension from beginning to end, but the heart of the book is its dollop of Sarah Dreher–style mysticism. It is also somewhat reminiscent

Visit us at www.boldstrokesbooks.com

Too Hot to Ride

by

Andrews & Austin

2020

TOO HOT TO RIDE

ISBN 13: 978-1-63555-776-3

THIS TRADE PAPERBACK ORIGINAL IS PUBLISHED BY
BOLD STROKES BOOKS, INC.
P.O. BOX 249
VALLEY FALLS, NY 12185

FIRST EDITION: SEPTEMBER 2020

CREDITS
EDITOR: SHELLEY THRASHER
PRODUCTION DESIGN: STACIA SEAMAN
COVER DESIGN BY TAMMY SEIDICK

Acknowledgments

Our love and thanks to our editor, Dr. Shelley Thrasher; BSB's former publicist and our friend, Connie Ward; our publisher, Rad; and the wonderful BSB team.

To all the women who "settled" in their relationships
and later found the courage to embrace the unsettling.

CHAPTER ONE

The unrelenting sun had dried ponds, cracked the earth, turned the ground to powder, and made everyone on the ranch flat-out irritable. I'd spent most of the summer sweat-soaked, and wrung out, and ready to make a deal with the devil if he'd put an end to the heat. The weatherman warned that a storm was brewing that could be tornadic. Nonetheless, I stood on the long plank porch staring north at the black wall cloud and begged it to move in and soak this lifeless prairie. I would far rather take my chances with a tempest than continue to dry up and blow away.

Cal, her hair matted from her riding helmet and perspiring head to toe in her jeans and boots, lumbered toward me to announce she'd canceled all the riding lessons for the day.

"Tried to get a few in early, but even the big fans in the arena can't move enough air to keep the kids from passing out."

"Everyone understand that?" I asked.

"Everyone but the ribbon junkies." Cal referenced the mothers who drove their little girls out to the ranch with visions of division trophies dancing in their heads. Cal had been in charge of the riding school for four years and knew riding herd on the mothers was far more difficult than teaching their kids to ride.

"Looks like we might get a break," I said, pointing to the wall cloud that was moving closer.

"Only if it blows Mrs. Windom to a different stable," she said, and I laughed. "God knows Sara Belle is bright and works hard, but I might as well be trying to teach a centipede to tap-dance. Constant hip-rolling and weight-shifting—she can make a perfectly trained horse stagger like a drunk."

"Well, Mrs. Windom is determined to turn her daughter into a horsewoman, so that means you're officially in hell—now, and for the foreseeable future."

"Well, thank you for that inspiring chat, Rae."

"Hey, raging hormones, constant tears and tantrums—it's got your name written all over it." Truth was I wouldn't work with preteen girls, mostly because I didn't want some sicko's accusation that I had an interest in their kid because I'm a lesbian. "You're the nice, motherly type who can deal with their drama, their periods, and their hysteria. You're the star of the show. I'm just the scenery," I said.

"Nice dust off," Cal replied.

I walked out onto the lawn to feel the full force of whatever meteorological mayhem was headed our way. The stables had cleared, and cars were trailing down the long drive as parents and their charges headed home to beat the storm.

Suddenly the wind picked up, blowing a heavy, brown Adirondack chair onto its side. A lead rope that one of the tiny equestrians had forgotten to hang on its hook skipped down the barn aisle. The temperature dropped thirty degrees, and the horses pricked up their ears, reared, and began to buck and cavort in the paddocks. As the storm began to blow through the ranch, shaking the trees and rattling windows, I smiled for the first time in a week.

Cal shouted to me from her refuge under the porch over-hang. "You'll be struck by lightning if you don't get over here!"

I looked back at the house with its tall wooden porch posts, big shuttered windows, and rustic rocking chairs with their cowboy cushions. How lucky I was to own this beautiful place—well, own it with the bank. A lightning bolt slammed into the ground nearby, sending off static electricity, and the hair on my arms stood up.

Cal shrieked at me again, "Are you trying to get killed?"

I bounded up onto the porch. The sound of the rain on the metal roof was loud yet comforting. I took a deep breath, enjoying the smell of the raindrops mingled with what was left of the dusty grass. We might get twenty-four hours of heat relief due to this downpour, and I'd gladly take it.

From our slightly elevated view, we could see the road in front of the ranch, and across it to another spread in the distance. Ranches dotted this part of the country, sitting far enough back off the road that you rarely saw the ranchers, yet close enough that they could come running in an emergency.

Suddenly, through the raging storm, a gray ghost train emerged, moving along the road in front of us. I squinted to make sure I was really seeing this drenched parade of vehicles.

"Looks like the circus has come to town," I said, with dark humor, as an entourage of horse trailers and SUVs moved past us like a mirage, plowed through the torrential rain, and pulled into the front gates of the ranch south of mine.

"Odd time for a real-estate showing," Cal said.

We both stared in the direction of the old, adjacent homestead that had been vacant for a year. If I'd had the money, I would have bought it. In fact, it used to be part of the land I now owned, but it was split off and sold decades before I arrived. Over the last four years, the ranch had traded hands multiple times, each owner less qualified than the last.

"I swear if someone's bought that place, I'm going to flip out."

"Well, someone needs to buy it before the weeds grow up over the windows." Cal stretched her neck to watch the trail of vehicles entering the front gates.

The Double Z Ranch was named after old man Zumwaldt, the rancher who became ill and had to sell it before I arrived. He was apparently the last person who knew anything about ranching. The next owner was a crooked developer who sold the land three times in a year, to three different people, tangling up the title, and we got in the habit of calling the ranch the Double Cross. An older couple turned it into a bed and breakfast, which we jokingly referred to as the Double Bed. Then a fella tried to turn it into a high-end trailer park, which we called the Double-Wide. And finally, it was a dude ranch, run by a dude who couldn't ride a horse, so we dubbed the place the Double-Dude. He'd abandoned the ranch almost on arrival, leaving it to the Johnson grass and rusting pipe… until today.

"That is one piece of beautiful dirt, and it deserves better than any of these rancher wannabes have given it," I said, disheartened and irritated that, once again, people might be moving in.

"Folks come and go, but the land stays put." Cal sighed, waxing philosophic.

"Every new owner just scars the place up worse than the last one, because all of them put together know less about ranching than this dog does." I gestured toward Hairy, who lay flat on the porch, and he let out a large groan, as if he didn't want to be compared to incompetents.

Ellie joined us on the porch to get a better view of the ranch to the south. "Not again," she said, referring to the possibility of more new neighbors.

Her lanky, teenage-boy frame and her short, dark hair made me wonder about her sexual preference, not that it was anyone's business. Cal thought she'd be a darling wife for a cute rancher, and I thought she'd be a cute partner for a good-looking woman. She was buoyant and pretty and could get people to tell her anything. In fact, she was the source of some of the best-ever equestrian-mother stories, which she liked to share with me on the porch at the end of the day.

"So what's going on with the clients?" I changed the subject, encouraging her to entertain us.

"Sara Belle's mother, Mrs. Windom, had two glasses of wine at the barn party and said her husband has erectile dysfunction. Can you believe she said that?" Ellie asked.

"Too much sharing." Cal scrunched her face up.

"And that redheaded lady, Mrs. Remington, Carolyne's mother, who always dresses like she's going to a dinner party…well, get this, she doesn't wear any underwear," Ellie reported.

"How do you know that?" I was amused.

"It was a really windy day." She gave it a beat. "Her real hair color is brown," Ellie added without cracking a smile.

"Well, since you're so good at getting the inside scoop, how about riding over to the Double Dude when the storm settles down to see who they are, and if they need any help?" "Need any help" was the calling card that got you onto a ranch to find out what the hell was going on.

"No problem," Ellie said, and immediately jogged off on her mission.

"I see you getting all tense." Cal eyed me. "Could be nothing. Maybe they've just rented the place for an event or something." About that time, a moving van came down the road and turned in. "Or maybe you're going to blow out through the top of your head." She jammed her straw fedora down on her mass of sandy-colored ringlets, making her look more like a coffeehouse musician than an accomplished horsewoman. "Just picked up the mail." Cal handed me a letter, along with a look that said be careful.

"Megan." I sighed, glancing at the Massachusetts return address. I tore the envelope open and scanned the letter quickly as Cal watched me, probably for signs of weakness. "Same old thing. Despite loving the tolerant, liberal East and hating the red, right-wing prairie, she misses me."

"Bullshit," Cal said, having no sympathy for infidelity since she'd fled California to rid herself of a drunken, unfaithful husband.

I tore up the letter and tossed the pieces into the trash. Cal walked off muttering, "Exactly where she belongs."

Five years of our lives with one another, I thought, yet Megan and I had never been in love. We'd needed each other the way the first two humans on Mars might: for companionship and survival—and for two liberal lesbians, Oklahoma felt like Mars. Whatever the reason, she'd tired of the heat, the oppression, and then it seemed we tired of each other. I bought her share of the ranch, which pretty much left me with not a lot more than the dirt under my feet.

The wind sent a chill across my chest. I looked down at my shirt, realizing I was storm-soaked from my vest to my boots, so I went inside to change, crossing the big living area with its faux-antler chandeliers and log pillars that replaced walls and implied a separation of rooms. The main room flowed into the kitchen, and the bedrooms were off to the side. On the south end of the house was a 20 x 30 office with its own southerly entrance and a porch that wrapped around the entire structure. The master was on the north wall, and that made the bedroom cool in summer, and still cooler in winter, which I became acutely aware of when my relationship ended.

I threw warm water on my face and splashed new makeup on, then ran a brush through my hair and blew my wet curls dry. *I'm doing okay for thirty-eight. Thinner from the breakup and the heat. Can't complain about thinner.* I leaned close to the makeup mirror to examine my hair for signs of blond giving way to premature gray. *Probably obsessing over gray hair because I was dumped.* My blue eyes, which people said went from dreamy to fiery in a blink, had lost a little of their sparkle, but then I hadn't had much to sparkle about lately.

Prowling through my closet for something dry to wear, I realized I looked like Ralph Lauren meets Scully—wall-to-wall leather pants, tailored jeans, starched white shirts, and several custom leather vests. *Kind of telegraphs my social life—horses and ranch work and not much else.* I threw on a clean white shirt and a thin leather vest with the RSR—Rae Starr Ranch—brand on it, brushed off my jeans and boots, and went back outside.

The storm had moved past and a coolness had settled over the ranch, so I plopped down on the porch swing that faced west to enjoy the peace and quiet, and the magnificent breeze that sent a chill up my arms. Cal rounded the corner from the stables, Ellie in tow. I could tell from the excitement playing just below her eyes, where the skin crinkled up when she was amused, that she was relishing whatever information they were about to drop on me.

"Well, Ellie went over there and met our new neighbor," Cal reported.

"So somebody bought the place?" I sighed, forlorn.

"Not exactly 'bought.' Tell her, Ellie."

Ellie cleared her throat as if about to give a high school presentation. "Well, the new owner is Ms. Jane Barrow, cutting-horse champion, and she won the ranch in a poker game."

"Sounds like we're gonna have to rename that ranch the Double or Nothin'." Cal grinned.

I vaulted out of the swing and landed two feet in front

of Ellie, who jumped back. "Some damned cowgirl won that ranch playing poker?"

"Not just any damned cowgirl, missy." Cal loved to tease me. "Jane Barrow. You should look her up. She was something in her day."

"In her day? So she's some old lady who's going to turn the place into a retirement home for busted bronc riders?"

Ellie rattled on at a rapid pace. "Said she was going to follow me back here, because she wanted to meet you in person, because she could tell from my visit that you were the type who had a lot of questions." Cal dragged Ellie away before she could end up in my blast furnace.

I was known for having a short fuse, which I'd tried to mature out of but so far wasn't making too much progress. I had a whole lot to be short-tempered about.

"I'm trying to run a damned riding school in a part of the country where summers mean 117-degree heat index, workers are crazy, right-wing Jesus freaks wear 'God Loves You' T-shirts while stealing everything that isn't bolted down, and every old white guy wants to know if I have a husband, because how else could I get enough money to buy a ranch, and that's before I have to deal with prepubescent little girls and their menopausal moms. And now this, with the ranch next door."

"Now, Rae. You get worked up every time it changes hands. They won't be over there long. None of them stay. So save your blood pressure," Cal said calmly.

"You know how many times I've planned and plotted to figure out a way to buy that spread, if for no other reason than to keep more weirdos from buying it? And now weirdo number five has beat me to it, and not even with hard-earned cash savings, but in some half-assed, cockamamie poker game. How can anyone value something they won in a damned poker game?" I said to Cal's backside as she headed for the barn, but mostly I was just venting into the air.

Before my steam had subsided, a big, tricked-out black King Ranch Expedition SUV pulled in through the open ranch gates, drove down the winding road, and parked just south of my office in front of the barn.

The door opened, and a tall, elegant woman, dressed in black, stepped out. She closed the door gently behind her, and in the sunlight I could see she had large, graceful hands that allowed her to wear an extra ring on her index finger. The ring glittered in the sunlight like trophy jewelry. Her black boots were silver wing-tipped, the shoulders of her tailored shirt were silver-trimmed, and her shiny silver hair was brushed back and just visible under the edge of her black cowboy hat. I'd never seen a woman look so good in a cowboy hat.

She tilted her aviator sunglasses down so I could see her eyes and said in a nice alto tone, "You must be Rae Starr." She extended her hand. "I'm Jane Barrow." She gave me a grin that damned near knocked me over. I kept looking into her eyes, which were absolutely gorgeous.

"You're a little bitty thing," she said. "You run this place all by yourself?"

"Size isn't a measure of competence," I shot back.

"True," she said good-naturedly, seeming amused by me, which made me bristle. "Since I'll be your neighbor, thought I'd stop by and say hello. We plan to run cutting horses, work with semi-pros who want to turn pro. I heard you've had your share of city folks moving in, so wanted to set your mind at ease that we know ranching. My ranch foreman is Wiley Evers, a good man. He can help you out if you ever need an extra hand in an emergency. I hope you'll stop by and pay me a visit some time."

"Did you really win that ranch in a poker game?" I didn't

even bother to work up to the question politely, too irritated that I wasn't the new owner.

"I did. I'm willing to take a gamble when I find something that's worth it." She winked at me. "Nice to meet you, Ms. Starr." Then Jane Barrow touched two long, elegant fingers to the brim of her hat, got into her SUV, and drove slowly down the ranch drive, heading south to her place.

Now that's one sexy damned woman. Wonder how old she is.

I went into my office, googled Jane Barrow Cutting Horse Champion, and found several dramatic shots of her on horseback going back two decades. One at a championship event in 2015, when she was forty-five. *So she's fifty now.* It was hard to believe the woman who got out of that SUV was fifty. *Well, good.* I let go of any romantic notions about glamorous cutting-horse champions. *Good that she's fifty.*

CHAPTER TWO

The heat had returned with such intensity that the wisteria on the front porch collapsed over the sides of their pots in surrender to the scorching sun. I spent my morning putting together internet flyers and electronic ads announcing Cal's western-dressage classes. I sent notifications to our more experienced riders about the upcoming shows and the registration requirements, then blasted out a mailing to everyone on our list, reminding them that horseback riding improves a rider's confidence and grace. Ellie interrupted me, saying there was a commotion in the arena.

"Sara Belle and Carolyne are in a major pissing contest. You better get over there right away."

I jumped up from my desk and hurried down the office steps past the wide barn aisle overlooking the south pastures, to the arena located down a dirt path east of the barn. Horse paddocks and grazing pastures were fenced off on the south and east. The layout was designed to make it easy to keep an eye on everyone and quicker to reach the horses and riders in an emergency. As I jogged along beside Ellie, she filled me in.

"Started two days ago. Cal thought she had them settled down, but Carolyne Remington has been needling Sara Belle pretty good, and now Sara Belle's threatening to slug her. I think she could deliver a pretty mean right hook."

Arriving minutes later in the arena, I could see the two little girls nose to nose. Carolyne, tall and thin, with perfect posture and every curl in place, was squared off with Sara Belle, who looked sloppy and perspiring and tear-stained. Cal was attempting to break up the fight.

"Hello, ladies!" My arrival startled them. "Too hot out to make things even hotter. What are we arguing about?"

"She called me a toad and said I'd never win anything, and I needed to find another sport and stop embarrassing myself," Sara Belle said defiantly, never taking her eyes off Carolyne. I looked at Carolyne for confirmation.

"I simply spoke the truth." Carolyne's private-school education came out in her calm, and succinct, fighting style. For just a second, I wondered if she knew her mother wore no underwear. The very fact that my mind went in that direction showed how much these kiddie altercations bored me.

"Today's truth is not always true tomorrow," I said quietly, and both of them blinked at me. "For example, as you probably know, people used to believe the earth was flat, and if you refuted that 'truth,' you would be executed. But now we know the earth is round. Well, at least most of us do. So yesterday's truth is no longer true. Therefore, the best approach is probably not to set ourselves up as truth tellers, but to work on our own skills and not judge others, because regardless of how good we are, someone will always be better. Handshake?" The girls reluctantly shook hands, then separated like prize fighters, going to opposite ends of the arena. *Probably waiting for me to leave so they can clobber each other.*

Cal whispered, "That was good."

"Only works because I rarely speak to them, so I'm a novelty." I headed back to the office, and over my shoulder I heard another little girl asking her mother why she had to share the arena with two riders who weren't as accomplished as she was. Her mother said she'd take that up with Cal. *Her mother should tell her to put a sock in it and get her ass on her pony and ride.* Puberty was difficult, but puberty on horseback was almost unbearable.

As I walked along the path back toward the house, I saw movement over on the south side of my ranch. Big cattle trucks were lumbering in, and young steers were being off-loaded. It looked like men were setting up chutes and water troughs for a cattle operation. Well, there are worse things, I thought. At the main entrance, two men were erecting a huge T-Bar and hanging a sign depicting a woman on a cutting horse and the words *Barrow Ranch*.

Late in the afternoon, the two ranch dogs, Hairy and Sally—stray mixed-breeds thoughtless people had dumped on our land—began howling like coyotes. Sally was a sweet, short, blond-fur dog, but I related more to Hairy's looks. His mass of gray, black, and white hair always stood straight up from his body like he'd just come from an electric shock treatment. *If I were a dog, that's how I would look—in a state of shock.* In fact I wasn't sure as a human that I wasn't starting to look that way. The two of them were howling in concert with a high-pitched sound it would take me another thirty seconds to hear…sirens.

The sirens grew louder and louder until they seemed to be on top of us. Cal and Ellie joined me, staring south toward the Barrow Ranch, where an ambulance wheeled in. The paramedics were there about half an hour, and then the ambulance slowly pulled away.

"Whatever it was, it can't have been that bad," I said to Cal. Had something happened to Jane? And why did I care, other than she seemed to add a little panache to the prairie?

"Want me to go find out?" Ellie seemed to be enjoying her role as riding-school spy.

"No. Let's not give them the impression we're monitoring their every move," I said, though frankly I was. "Unless you're interested in something over there." I was teasing Ellie, and she blushed.

"Nothing I want." She blew out a puff of air, sounding like an irritated horse.

❖

Later that afternoon, the farrier arrived to shoe our six stable horses. Some of the boarders brought in their own farrier, but most used ours, which meant he had about a dozen horses to trim every six weeks. He'd spent the morning at the Barrow Ranch, shoeing a few of their horses—grouping his ranch clients to save time and money—and he mentioned he was there when the ambulance arrived.

"She had some workers putting up the chutes, and one of them got his hand slammed in the slide and crushed it. Took him in for X-rays, that kind of thing." The farrier, a short, stocky, ruddy-faced man, chewed tobacco as he worked.

"Lose any fingers?" I asked.

"Don't think so, but doubt he'll be playin' the violin any time soon," he replied, whittling on a hoof as he spoke and spat.

"Did he play the violin before?" I grinned, playing along with the old joke.

"Nope." We both laughed.

"So what do you think about that?" I asked. Farriers were the hairdressers of the horse world. They knew everybody, and everything, and giving him an open-ended question was like asking, "So what did you find out?"

"From what I hear, she's the real deal. Knows her stuff,

been around—not a bad lady." He paused to spit his chaw. "Bit of a rounder, I guess, in her youth."

"How round?" I poked fun at his description of her.

"Let's just say, word is she's had a lot of shoes under her bed." He chuckled.

"Nothin' wrong with that, I guess."

"Of all sizes." He laughed again, and I wondered if he was trying to say she was bisexual, but I changed the subject, knowing there's a point where folks in the country think you've gone from joshing to prying.

"Check Bellamy's feet, will you?" I focused on the big, black lesson horse he was trimming. "Seems like he's stabbing that right front into the ground."

"Will do. Heat and temperature shifts causing a lot of tender feet this summer."

"Last year it was rich grass, this year heat stress. 'Healthy as a horse' is a joke. If you see any early sign of foundering, go ahead and put him in the third stall." I thanked him, thinking I'd like to go to the Barrow Ranch and see what she was up to. *Must be the "shoes of all sizes" that has me curious.*

I enjoyed conversations with the farrier and the other cowboys who came and went out here on the ranch. Although I'd gone to school back East, I was an Okie at heart and loved the vivid language of the prairie. The farrier glanced up from his work. "Tried the new bakery."

"How'd you like it?"

"Get one of those death-by-chocolate, double-fudge thingies. Richer than three foot up a bull's butt." He whistled in appreciation, and I laughed.

"Well now, that's a highly visual recommendation. I'll try one," I said and went back to my office.

I'd barely gotten settled at my desk when a tap on my

office window and Margaret Windom's face peering through the glass startled me. I hated it when mothers skipped Cal and came to see me about their kids, and I particularly hated it when Margaret Windom visited me, because she made me uncomfortable. She was about my height, with short, dark hair brushed forward framing her face, and she wore almost military-style dresses with cinched waists and epaulets that made her appear even more domineering than she was. If I let my mind run free, which was never a good idea, my mind would be fleeing the building right now.

For two years, Margaret Windom barely knew I was alive, but in the chaos of my breakup, during which Megan flitted around the barn aisles like an aggrieved drama queen, Margaret must have realized that Megan and I might be more than just roommates, and that revelation seemed to pique her interest. Recently, I noticed her interest had turned to something more personal I didn't want to think about, because she followed me with her gaze as if she were a peregrine falcon and I a field mouse.

I opened the door and asked her in, offering her a place to perch. "I don't want to interrupt," she said, having already interrupted, "but I heard from Sara Belle that she had a little altercation with a fellow rider."

"I think it all got resolved. It's the heat. Sometimes tempers flare."

"She said you intervened and made her feel better, and I wanted to thank you personally."

"You're welcome," I said, in a tone that I hoped indicated finality.

"I wish you were teaching Sara Belle. She would go farther so much faster. Don't get me wrong. I like Cal, she is a dear, but she's not you."

"Well, that's very kind, but I'm not an instructor."

"I think instruction is an attitude, not a plaque on the wall. I would be willing to compensate you above and beyond what you would require," she said, and placed her hand on mine, then left it there. After a beat, I slid my hand away.

"If I were to work with Sara Belle, then I would have to work with other girls as well, and it's just not something I can do right now." *Or ever!* I wanted to shout.

"Would you be open to conversations with me about her, over dinner perhaps, to help me help her?" I could see the shift in her facial expression and knew we were heading into dangerous waters. I didn't want to be in the water with any student's mother, least of all Margaret Windom. "Think about that, and we'll talk again," she said, seeming to sense me tensing up. "Meanwhile, I'll ask Cal to double up on her lessons." Margaret left, having dangled more money, via more lessons, and I was sure she flipped her derriere toward me, in a playful way, as she exited. It was not attractive. Where is Mr. Windom these days while his wife is flirting with, and flipping her fanny at, the ranch owner? I wondered. Probably off with his secretary and not giving a shit.

Poor Cal—double lessons with Sara Belle. Poor me—in the crosshairs of her mother.

CHAPTER THREE

C al had a western-dressage background, which was a discipline that combined western tack and cowboy riding stock with classical dressage moves, leaving room for the horses to express themselves in keeping with their breed. Western dressage allowed more young women who came from roping and riding, or barrel-racing backgrounds, to show off the versatility of their horses. Cal trained western dressage, levels one through three, on Tuesday through Friday after school. Then, early mornings and Saturdays in particular, the barn was awash in young beginners who rode the stable horses and learned the basics of riding and how to care for a horse.

We had not only a wide range of skill sets, but also a wide range of ages. I constantly heard Cal reminding the smallest among them to pick up their feed buckets, hang on to their horse's lead rope, and watch where they were stepping. While Cal didn't exclude young boys, the sport attracted far more girls, because they intuitively understood the horses. Girls from an early age related to a horse's sensitivity and gentleness, when handled correctly, and they seemed to bond more readily with the big animals.

It was Tuesday late in the day when I accidentally bumped into Margaret Windom, having forgotten she'd doubled down on Sara Belle's lessons. She strode over to me wearing riding breeches, a riding crop tucked under her arm, looking as if she'd just parked her panzer division at the gate. *Sex with her must be painful. Probably takes the crop to bed.*

"I'm so glad I ran into you," she said, keeping one eye on Sara Belle as Cal worked with her in the dressage ring. "Don't you think Sara Belle is ready to move up to level 2? She's obviously improved dramatically."

You got to love mothers, I thought. Margaret is looking at her kid, who's built like a Bartlett pear, and who couldn't "turn on the forehand" if the forehand had a knob, and she's telling me Sara Belle is ready for the next level. "I think you and I should leave that up to Cal and Sara Belle," I said, as courteously as I could muster.

"You're right," she said, and I was sure she was suppressing the desire to say I wasn't and discipline me with her riding crop. "How about dinner sometime, just you and me? At my home. My husband travels all over the world, so he's rarely there."

"Mrs. Windom, that is so kind—"

"Call me Margaret."

"I just don't socialize with my clients, because it favors one parent over another, and because I'm just so busy."

"That's too bad, because I'm a parent worth favoring." She moved ten feet to her right, distancing herself from me, and spoke over her shoulder. "I'll let you go, because I know how busy you must be," she said, with just a hint of sarcasm, insulting my productivity and making me feel like a hood ornament on my own ranch.

❖

I was working on the books when Cal came up to the house at the end of the day and sat down on the porch. I took a break and handed her a cold beer from the mini-fridge in the office.

"Saw you got trapped by Mommy Dearest."

"Woman creeps me out," I said. "She's trying to get me to have dinner with her alone."

Cal imitated Ray Stevens in *The Streak.* "Don't do it, Ethel!"

"Are you kidding me. Of course not!"

"She's so condescending, I want to slap her. No wonder her poor kid is like a skittish colt, never wanting to get on the wrong side of her." We both sat for a while, the heat still unbearable, but the hot breeze blowing across our sweat-stained shirts provided some comfort.

"We doing the right thing, Cal, with the ranch and all?" I asked, a bit melancholy.

"Long as one of us doesn't fall over and die, yeah."

"Well, that was comforting. Thanks." I snorted.

"What else would we be doing, Rae? We're making a living. Twenty years from now, these kids will own a horse, or be taking their kids for lessons, because they'll remember what they experienced here and what horses meant to their lives. So we do it for the kids, and we do it for the horses. The mothers, well—it's the price we pay."

"Okay. Just checking."

"You going over to see your neighbor?" Cal asked, like a mother trying to find something for a bored child to do.

"Why would I?"

"Why wouldn't you? She's interesting." Cal slugged down her beer, and we both sat in the quiet. Cal tended to calm me down. She could sit for hours and say nothing, which was kind of comforting to a person like me, who had trouble sitting still ten minutes and felt I'd have plenty of time to be silent once I was dead.

"Maybe I will," I said. "Later, when I have time."

Cal shot me a look. "Find time. You need a play date. You've been about as much fun lately as an enema."

I laughed in spite of myself.

❖

It was ten o'clock at night, and while we didn't have any clients to complain about the sound, the raucous music from the Barrow Ranch echoed across mine. My hackles went up. I had watched them erect several tall poles earlier in the afternoon, and then they'd attached something to them. It hadn't dawned on me that they were hanging loudspeakers on them, and now they were broadcasting rock music. My blood pressure shot up, and I was just about to go over and tell them this had to stop, when it ceased on its own. The silence momentarily calmed me. Maybe they're just testing some equipment, I thought. Surely they don't think they get to own the airspace for a mile around.

❖

At ten o'clock the next morning, the music came on suddenly, and at high volume, blasting through the air. It startled the three little girls in the beginners' class, who were taking an early morning lesson, and they immediately became hysterical, behaving as if someone had just dropped a bomb in their midst. Their panic panicked their horses, and Cal had to deal with twelve-hundred-pound animals skittering across the arena, which brought more screams from the girls, who struggled not to fall off. Then a loud male voice blasted over the PA. "Ladies and gentlemen, welcome to the cutting-horse finals. First up on Rocket-In-Your-Pocket, owned by Valenti Stables and ridden by Jaimie Valenti…"

Rachel, an eight-year-old rider in pigtails, whose father was an evangelical preacher, stared up at the ceiling, as if the booming male voice signaled the end of days.

Cal quickly picked up a microphone and switched it on. "Ladies, everyone to the center of the ring. Take a deep breath. There you go. Relax, and relaaax your horses. Now, one at a time, beginning with Rachel, we will dismount. This is excellent training, as many unexpected events occur at horse shows."

Before she'd gotten everyone to dismount, I was in my truck, headed for the Barrow Ranch.

I wheeled into the driveway spraying gravel, signaling my discontent before ever stepping out of my vehicle. A short, buffed, middle-aged cowboy dressed in a snappy cowboy shirt and pressed jeans stepped up to greet me and introduced himself as Wiley Evers. I could have sworn he was suppressing a chuckle as I worked up a head of steam.

"Are you aware that your sound system is about three thousand decibels too loud and scaring the hell out of my students and their horses?" I said.

The ranch house door opened, and Jane Barrow stepped out on her porch wearing a pair of worn blue jeans that came down over the top of her blue Lucchese exotics, a pale-blue work shirt open over a blue tee, and flashing her championship belt buckle and that smile.

She greeted me. "I was hoping you'd come visit."

"She's here about the PA system scarin' the little girls." Wiley stared at the dirt. I was certain he was looking at the ground, rather than at me, so I couldn't see his expression. *If he's grinning, I'm going to slap that smirk right off him.*

"We try to create an environment as much like the show environment as possible." Jane Barrow took her hat off and scratched the back of her head, and her silver hair looked beautiful. I wondered how she managed not to have hat-hair.

"That's interesting, but I've got my own set of problems," I said. "If some little girl has an accident because she and her horse freak over these audio blasts, I could have a lawsuit."

"I understand," Jane said.

"Here's the deal. You own your real estate with the air above and the ground below, but you don't own *all* the air, and certainly not the air above my place, so drop those speakers down level with the arena and cut the volume back, or I'll have to report you."

"To who?" she asked in a serious tone, her brow furrowed.

"To whoever fines people like you."

"Ms. Starr, no offense, but you kind of shoot first and ask questions later. You had me handcuffed at hello. Let me see what I can do. I want us to be neighborly."

I turned and stormed off to let her know I meant business. Wiley let out a whistle behind my back. "High-strung" was what he called me. I whirled back around.

"And give me your phone number, so I can call next time and don't have to drive over here."

Jane reached into her shirt pocket and pulled out a printed business card that said *Barrow Ranch*, with a photo of her in action on a cutting horse. "Call me any time," she said, and her politeness kind of deflated my anger. "Better yet, would you like to have lunch with me? Wiley's a real good cook, and I think he'd be happy to share with us. That way, we could get to know each other a little bit, and I could sleep nights not having to worry that every time you show up, you're gonna pull a knife on me." She gave me a grin.

"It's only ten thirty," I said, caught off guard.

"Yeah. You'd have to come back or just stay over. How about, say, noon?" I nodded before I caught myself. "Anything you're allergic to, other than loud music?"

She was charming and irrepressible. I squinted at her and pursed my lips, and she laughed. "Wiley, you're on! The lady's agreed to lunch."

I walked to my truck and drove back to my ranch, where Cal stood waiting, having finished with the girls. "Did you tell her she nearly caused a train wreck? One of those girls has been on a horse only twice in her life." Cal laughed. "That poor Rachel comes from a real evangelical family, and I'm pretty sure she thought that disembodied voice booming overhead meant we were about to be caught up in the Rapture."

"I told Jane to lower the speakers and cut the sound back."

"And what did 'Jane' say?"

"She asked me to have lunch with her at noon."

Cal looked like she had a lot to say but was saving it up for another time. "That's good, I guess. Wonder if lunch will have musical accompaniment."

CHAPTER FOUR

The blue place mats had images of a dark horse on them, and the silverware handles were shaped like a horse head. The circular porch table set for two, with white plates and tea glasses, overlooked the back pond, which was more secluded than the front of the ranch house. Off to the side, Wiley, in a chef's apron, grilled burgers, as Jane offered me a seat.

"This is such a pretty place," I said quietly. "I always dreamed of recombining the two ranches like the original homestead, but I keep missing my chance." Maybe it was my way of explaining the fervor of my last visit and my less-than-cordial tone.

"What brought you out here?" she asked.

"More land for less money. The idea of coming back to my roots," I said. She was paying attention like she was really interested. "I don't mean to harp on this, but you just pulled up stakes and moved to Oklahoma because you won a ranch in a card game."

"You can't imagine doing that?"

"I'm not a gambler."

"You're in a red, religious, right-wing state, on a ranch alone, training horses, and teaching kids to ride huge animals that could trample them. You're a gambler." She raised her tea glass, and we toasted my heretofore unrecognized gambling streak.

Wiley swooped the burgers, already in their buns, onto our plates and placed a bowl of potato salad and one with cole slaw on the table. I took a bite and complimented him.

"There were years I think she only kept me because I could cook," he joked.

"It was a draw between his cooking and his charming personality," Jane said, her tone playful, and I realized she was at ease with men as much as she was with women…leading my mind back to the shoe sizes under her bed.

I ate my burger, glancing at Jane whenever I thought she wouldn't notice. *She even looks good while she's eating.* She was just, well, cool.

"JB, you through with me?" Wiley asked to be relieved of his chef duties. I had a feeling he'd jumped in to help, knowing it was important to get me on their side so we didn't have a ranch war.

"Great job, on short notice. Thank you, Mr. Evers," Jane said, and he shut the grill down and moved on to his ranch duties.

Jane gestured toward the potato salad, asking me if I'd like some. She didn't pick up the bowl or try to serve me, just gestured in that direction, which kind of amused me. Jane Barrow was obviously used to people serving her, and she was no one's little hostess. She'd even outsourced cooking a hamburger to Wiley.

"So do you cook?" I couldn't resist digging her just a little.

"You mean if Wiley quit, would I starve to death? Absolutely. Can't fry an egg, make a sandwich, or barbecue a steak. I'm helpless." Her tone mocked me, and I smirked. "Can *you* cook?"

"I'm good at it."

"So maybe you'll invite me to dinner." She grinned. "Or we could just start having lunch over here every day, and then dinner at your place." She was toying with me and obviously enjoying it, so I ignored the remark.

"Word is, you've had a pretty wild life," I said.

"You say that like you think it's over. How old are you?"

"I'll be thirty-nine."

"So you're thirty-eight." She might as well have said, That explains a lot. "And you're single. Have you always been single?"

"If you mean was I ever married— "

"I mean did you ever have a live-in lover, a partner?"

"I did. We broke up, and she went back to Massachusetts two years ago. We were together five years." Jane didn't react to my confessed lesbianism.

"Was that fine with you?"

"Yeah, actually, it was, in hindsight. I wasn't too happy about it at the time." I was uncomfortable by the way she fired questions at me and began to squirm in my seat. "I think it's my turn to ask a few questions. You seem interested in who's loving who, so are you in love with anyone now?"

She chuckled. "Now that's a much better question than mine."

My phone rang, and, exasperated, I glanced down to see who it was. Cal's name popped up, and I knew I'd better take it, because she never interrupted unless it was an emergency. I apologized to Jane, saying I wanted to make sure one of the riders hadn't been injured. She studied me the entire time I was on the phone, as if taking my measure, formulating an opinion about me.

Meanwhile, coming across the phone line was a barrage

of information, invading my lunch with Jane, forcing me to focus away from her. Finally, I found a spot in Cal's monologue where I could interrupt.

"Cal, I don't think that's a good thing to do." I paused as she rattled on. "I know, but we're not in the rescue business. We have clients and—" Cal interrupted again, so I told her I'd come back to the ranch and discuss it with her in person.

"Sorry," I said to Jane after I hung up. "Cal got a call asking us to take some slaughter horses a friend rescued. Cal's tender-hearted and always wants to drag home any bag of bones she finds. I feel sorry for them, but they're money out the door, they can bring disease to your other horses, and they require around-the-clock rehab. I just don't feel I can take them on."

"And sometimes they can turn out to be the best horse in your stable, because they're so damned grateful. Personally, I think they're worth the gamble. How many do they want you to take?"

"Three that kinda stuck together."

"Tell you what, if you see your way clear to do it, I'll help you with it. My word," she said, and extended her hand. I put my hand in hers, and I had to keep myself from shivering. Jane Barrow had big energy and, apparently, a big heart. "Call me when you bring them in, and I'll be over," she said, already assuming she'd sold me.

I bid Jane Barrow good-bye, thanking her for the lunch and wishing I didn't have to leave. Of all the damned times for Cal to have to interrupt me, she picks today while I'm having lunch with Jane Barrow. I swear I'm tortured and can't get a break.

I whipped my old red, short-bed Silverado into the ranch drive and jumped out. Cal was waiting for me, pacing and saying the friends who'd called needed an answer. The truth was, I could barely stand to see the condition of the horses that were pulled from slaughter and preferred to donate money to others to help their rescue efforts. I couldn't imagine the courage it took to go to the kill pens, where a few horses would be singled out and saved, the rest chopped up in the most horrific fashion. The terror in their eyes as they begged to be rescued haunted me. They'd ended up in this situation because breeders overbred, searching for the next Secretariat, and owners often pulled the losers right off the race track, then handed them over to the kill buyers, where they were jammed onto trucks without food or water and driven to Mexico or Canada to slaughterhouses. They ended up there also because families couldn't feed them. Or worse, they were four-year-olds and perfectly healthy, but no longer tax-deductible, so the owners and breeders killed that crop and bred again. I could hardly stand to think about it, but Cal was in front of me begging me to reconsider.

"Okay," I finally said. "Get the vet and have them checked for equine HIV and anything else they might give our horses. If we make a mistake and one of them is contagious, we'd have to put down every horse on the property, and our business would be bankrupt."

Cal gave me a huge hug, which was unlike her, and it brought tears to my eyes. "They've already been tested. They're transporting them pretty quick, because they're in such bad shape. They'll have them here tomorrow morning."

"Let's shuffle the horses around and create a paddock downwind of the other horses, and get a round bale loaded in there. They'll have water and a shed for shade. And tell the students these horses are off-limits, because we don't know how socialized they are or what they're carrying."

I didn't know why I was taking this burden on. I had the heart for it always, but often fear overtook me. Maybe it was having Jane Barrow's word that she stood ready to help.

CHAPTER FIVE

By morning, we were all nervously waiting for the horse trailer that finally bounced down the drive and over to the back pasture, where I directed the driver to pull in. It was a metal-slat, low-end, transport trailer, being hauled by a rusty, old, blue-and-white Ford pickup, which jerked through the gate and stopped. It didn't have any compartments or tie-downs for the three horses that were jammed into the small space, and they lurched around inside. Theoretically, this was first-class transportation, since they'd just escaped execution.

I glimpsed the animals inside—two whites and a bay. The driver slung the back door open. The horses looked wary and skinny, their heads huge and bony. They reminded me of animal parts found in archeological digs—skeletons with skin stretched over them. But that wasn't as bad as their bony, pathetic bodies, with the hips sunken in and rib cages sticking out. The driver walked in, dodging the bay, and hooked up the two whites and led them out, unsnapping the halter leads and turning them loose in the pasture.

One mare immediately went down on her knee, and we rushed to pull her up and steady her. I felt her leg, but she didn't wince. She stood blinking and looking around, and we slowly walked her toward the hay bale. The driver went back for the bay, and she backed herself up into the front of the trailer and let him know she wasn't cooperating, and he was the one who'd better leave. Despite the animal's fear, and hunger, and fatigue, she gave the poor man a workout—backing up, whipping around in the trailer, and slamming her hooves up against the metal wall. I didn't blame her. Where she'd been, what she'd seen, and having narrowly escaped a horrible death would make any living creature furious.

It took the driver three tries before he could get her out, and when he let her loose in the pasture, she bucked and kicked a few times before planting her nose in the hay. The two white mares ignored her, as if numb to any further drama. The driver waved and got back in his truck, saying he had to hightail it back to the ranch where the rest of the battered horses were penned up, awaiting transport to whoever would help by taking them.

The white mares looked so weak I didn't know if we'd gotten them in time. The intense heat wasn't helping, and frankly, I didn't even know if these horses had the energy to flick the flies off themselves, so I asked Ellie to move some of the school horses around to free up two stalls at one end of the barn, where they'd have a breeze and water-fans, and we could isolate them from the other horses.

While she was rearranging the barn stalls, I hung over the fence with Cal, watching the three rescue mares.

"A couple of the little girls heard they were coming and named them in absentia. The two white horses are Snow White and Sleeping Beauty. Snow and Beauty for short," Cal informed me, saying Snow had flecks of gray on her nose, and that's how I was supposed to know the difference.

"I'm naming the bay mare Howie," Cal added.

"That's a terrible name for a mare," I said.

"Fits." She grinned. "Howie gonna get hold of her to trim

her hooves? Howie gonna give her meds without being killed? Howie ever gonna ride her?"

"Yeah, you're right. Good name," I said.

The vet was due to look them over, and half an hour later, his old tech truck pulled into the drive and he stepped out—tall and lean, a slow-talking, no-frills fella who'd been working ranch horses for decades. He shouted out a lively greeting, tipping back his summer Stetson with the sweat stains now permanently pressed into the headband. He wiped his hands on the back of his baggy jeans and asked where the rescue horses were. I indicated the pasture right off the south end of the barn.

"We can bring up the two white mares, Beauty and Snow, but Howie is a challenge," I said.

The vet was already walking in their direction, obviously curious what condition they were in. "They got their halters on. That's good. Let's snap on a lead rope and bring 'em on up, so I can have a look."

Cal hooked up the two white mares and slowly walked them out. They were sweet and kind in spite of all the atrocities human beings had inflicted on them. Snow was the mare that had gone down on her knee, and she limped after that, signaling a problem. Once Cal had the two mares out, the vet walked into the pasture where Howie remained. "Let's see about you, big girl."

Howie was a big, beautiful bay with a reddish-brown body and jet-black mane and tail, and you could see that with care and the right nutrition, her coat might glisten and her mane fill out. However, Howie had decided that, with the possible exception of Snow and Beauty, this was now her territory, and she wasn't up for a spa day. She'd closed the door to anyone else entering her pasture, but she was clever about it. Instead of shying away like most horses would have when facing a stranger, Howie came right at the vet and slid to a stop in front of him, as if she was glad to meet him. He extended his hand to touch her, and Howie reared up on her hind legs and paddled her front hooves over his head, striking at him. He leapt back and practically vaulted out of the pasture. *Did a man own and abuse Howie?* She'd let Cal walk into her pasture to get the white mares, but she hadn't given the male transport driver and male vet a warm welcome.

"That's not a happy mare," the vet announced, which was an understatement. A horse paddling above your head can bring a hoof down and kill you in an instant. Howie's behavior could mean she was frightened, or had no respect for humans, or it could be a sign of some mental instability that would mean putting her down. She'd managed to avoid the ravages of weight loss the white mares had suffered, but her temperament might have gotten her sent to the kill buyer.

"How are we going to vet her?" I asked.

"If I could get close enough, I could shoot her with a sedative. Doesn't look like she's going to tolerate that today. I'd leave her alone and not worry about the vetting for a few days. I don't even know that I'd let anyone really mess with her who doesn't know horses," he said, and I was pretty sure that was his escape speech. He didn't want to work with Howie.

The vet gave Beauty and Snow their exams in the barn aisle. They stood like big war horses, battered and worried, as he examined chest, hooves, eyes, and teeth. "Look to be about twelve or thirteen, from their teeth. Sixteen hands and probably Arab mix. Since no one'll be riding them, no need to subject them to any tooth filing or that kind of thing. This one with the limp, let's put her on bute for a couple of days, but give her some Ulcergard first to protect her stomach, because I imagine she's got nothing in her. Looks like they starved her long before they decided to toss her."

"I'd truly like to take a gun and shoot the people who did this to these poor animals. No, first I'd like to starve them and then shoot them," I said.

"It can make you pretty mad," he acknowledged. "We'll take the pain away and see if she'll walk on that hoof better. If not, let me know, and we'll X-ray. Sweet horses. Now that other one out there," he jerked his thumb in the direction of Howie, "maybe fifteen and a half hands, looks to be all quarter horse, and hell on wheels." He laughed, but we both knew she could be dangerous.

Cal spoke up as the vet was driving off. "Guess we need a plan for Howie."

"Got any ideas?" I asked.

We looked down the barn aisle, through the open barn doors to the south pasture where Howie was snorting and screaming and bucking.

"Think maybe she's in some kind of pain?" Cal asked.

"You go ahead and examine her. I'll be right behind you," I joked.

The big, black Expedition pulled through the gates, interrupting our conversation, and Jane and Wiley stepped out. Jane's voice boomed. "Heard the rescues arrived."

I stepped up to greet the two of them. "Two white mares are right there in the last two stalls, really kind animals," I said.

We all followed Jane as she walked down the long barn aisle, past the feed room, and the barn office, and the wash bay, stopping at the two mares' stalls. She put her hand out, rubbing their muzzles and addressing the horses. "You two are in serious need of some groceries," she whispered. Then she turned to look at me, sadness in her eyes. "How the hell can people treat animals like this?"

"When they sell the animal to a kill buyer, and he drives away with the horse, the owner gets his fifty bucks and never has to see the anguish and terror the horse goes through. For him, it's all done, problem solved—tidy, over with, and he can get back to what's for dinner." I realized I was lecturing, so I stopped, but Jane kept looking at me, kind of like she was reaching a conclusion about me, and her staring made me shy.

I could tell Cal liked Jane right away, and I introduced everyone. I thought I caught Cal taking an extra-long look at Wiley, who was trim and muscled and handsome, if you were into middle-aged cowboys. I had to admit he did have pretty blue eyes.

"Thought you said there was three?" Wiley said.

"Third one is Howie, the mare from hell," Cal replied.

"Can I have a look?" Wiley asked, and Cal seemed more than anxious to walk him to Howie's pasture. I noticed as they strode off together that Wiley was medium build, not very tall, but wedge-shaped. His broad shoulders triangled down to his tight little cowboy ass. He was no drugstore cowboy, that was for sure.

Alone in the barn aisle with Jane, I felt self-conscious for no apparent reason, so I focused on the horses, stroking Beauty's big, soft muzzle. "I have to look twice to figure out which of them is Snow and which is Beauty. This one's Snow," I said, and Jane walked closer, hanging her hand over Snow's stall, close to my arm. We were both quiet after that.

"Sound system still bothering you?" she finally asked.

"We can still hear it," I said, and she nodded.

She was maybe four inches taller than me, taller still in her hat. Standing alone with her in such close proximity, something inside me began to shift and heat up. I hadn't had that feeling for a long time. *No question. I'm physically attracted to her.*

Suddenly out of nowhere she asked, "How tall are you lying down?"

I was startled and then burst out laughing. "Whaaat?"

She must have realized that sounded suggestive, and she apologized. "That's just my way of saying…you know, how tall are you without your boots on?"

"I'm five foot four."

"No, you're not."

"Well, five foot three," I admitted.

"If you stand up real tall."

"And you need this information because…" I bristled.

"I'm just gathering data. Nothing to worry about. Your personal information is safe with me and will never be hacked or breached. Although I may reserve the right to sell the data regarding your height to third parties, so they can send you dozens of unwanted emails, trying to sell you growth supplements."

I laughed, and we stared at one another for a moment before Wiley and Cal came through the barn door.

"JB, I think you might want to come take a look at this bay," Wiley said with more energy than I remembered him having left with, and Cal looked pretty energized herself.

We both followed Wiley back to the pasture and hung over the pipe rail, as Wiley slowly let himself into the paddock. Despite the mare's attitude and being slightly underweight, her charisma was unmistakable.

"Wiley, don't get in there and get yourself hurt!" I said loudly. But Wiley was focused on the horse.

"Don't worry about him," Jane said. "In addition to his culinary skills, he's a damned good jumper, and he'll clear that fence if he needs to."

Howie reared up and pawed the air, as she had with the vet, but Wiley stepped out of her way, locked eyes with her, and began to dodge back and forth in front of her, like he was playing with her. She put her front feet down, made a move as if about to play in return, then spun, showing him her butt, and took off across the pasture. Wiley walked out of the paddock.

"Need a lot of work," he said, looking at Jane.

Jane turned to me. "Do you have anyone here who wants to work with this horse? Because if you don't, I'd like to buy her from you."

"And do what with her?" I asked.

"I don't know, exactly."

"You want to buy her, and you don't know why or what you're going to do with her?"

Jane pushed her hat back and stared at me with those gorgeous hazel eyes, and the crow's-feet at the edges just made her look sexier. "You're a woman who has to button everything down, aren't you? Okay, I'm going to turn her into a riding horse…my personal riding horse."

I whooped a little too loudly over that remark, and Wiley's grin was billboard-sized.

"I'll socialize her, and once she's sound, I'll have a saddle on her and ride her a week after that." I rolled my eyes, and Jane grinned. "You don't believe me." About that time, Howie went on the biggest tear we'd seen to date—kicking, and snorting, showing her teeth and screaming. It was as if the horse was weighing in on Jane's comments, letting her know hell would freeze over before she became anyone's riding horse.

I couldn't stop laughing. Rather than being offended, Jane seemed amused. "Wiley, I can see that this is going to require a wager." She grinned at me. "Rae Starr, let's make a bet. Wiley, you got a pen and something to write on?"

Wiley dug around in his pockets until he found a pen and the back of an old scrap of paper. Jane tore it in two and gave me half. "Okay, the bet is I ride her a week after the vet says she's sound. You write down what I have to do if I fail to do that, and I will write down what you have to do, if I do what I say. Short of selling or forfeiting our ranches, name what you want." I scribbled something, while Jane wrote deliberately. "Now, Cal, do you have an envelope?" Jane asked. Cal ducked into the barn office to get one. "Cal is going to seal up our demands in this envelope, and the winner will be announced one week after the vet pronounces Howie sound enough to be ridden."

"The vet may not be able to get a hand on Howie," I said.

"Well then, you would win," Jane replied.

"And you have to stay on her to win. You can't fall off," I said.

Wiley began to chuckle, and Jane played to him.

"The woman thinks I'll fall off," she said, suppressing a smile.

"Well, I have seen that happen." Wiley grinned.

Jane turned back to me. "Is three hundred a fair price for Howie?"

"I'll give you Howie."

"Nope. I'll buy her fair and square. And I'll want to move her over to my place."

"No. Leaving the white mares is too traumatic. They're her buddies. You'll have to work her over here. But you have to sign a waiver that, if either of you are injured or killed, it's not on me. I don't want any lawsuits. And you have to keep Howie away from the kids."

Jane let all the air out of her jaws. Wiley shot her a playful look, as if to say I was a handful to deal with, and Jane shook her head, as if they were both about to get themselves into something they might regret.

"Okay, but I pay no rent, just feed, and vet, and anything the horse needs. I'd also like everyone to stay away from her for a while, except Wiley and me," Jane said, extending her hand and enveloping mine. Her grip was firm but her hand surprisingly soft. She held me in her grasp for just a moment longer than was necessary to consummate a bet, and just long enough to increase my heart rate. Jane Barrow had a wonderful handshake.

CHAPTER SIX

The heat was so oppressive we couldn't breathe. The intermittent rain had cooled things off temporarily, but when the sun came out, again topping a hundred degrees and no breeze, the entire prairie turned into a sauna. We checked the horses daily to make sure they had water and shade, salt blocks to make them drink, and mineral blocks to balance their electrolytes, and of course we monitored them to be sure they weren't showing signs of stress—which could look like labored breathing, muzzles drawn up in wrinkles around their nostrils, or hot hooves. Nonetheless, they were drenched around their flanks and bellies and around their eyes and under their manes. They were miserable. Hosing down horses who were standing in the sun was just baking them and making them hotter, so we had to rely on their natural cooling system: sweat and a breeze.

But we did hose down Beauty and Snow and put them in the arena, then turned the fans on. They were already so frail and thin, we didn't want heat stress to make things worse. Some of the horses were under the trees and a few in their stalls with water fans that blew mist on them. Howie, on the other hand, wasn't letting anyone near her to help. She was panting and baking, but threatening anyone who tried to approach her. She had us worried.

Just when I was about to call Wiley, he and Jane came over pulling a horse trailer with a picture of a black quarter horse on it and *Dark Horse* painted on the big, sleek sides. The black horse inside was tacked up, and he backed down the ramp like a gentleman, ready to ride. Jane raised her hand to me, by way of greeting, and then went about helping Wiley, while I watched from the rails, and Cal joined me.

Even on the ground, Jane Barrow moved with confidence, as if she knew exactly what she was going to do and how she planned to do it. Years of winning must have instilled success in her DNA. I couldn't imagine that she ever let herself think "what if I lose," or "what if I get hurt," or "what if this turns out to be wrong." She was all confidence, and I found that extremely sexy.

Dark Horse nuzzled her and seemed to have more affinity for her than Wiley, although he was a gentleman to everyone. And you could tell that Jane was very fond of him, because she cuddled his head and scratched his cheek and whispered into his ear.

Finally, Wiley came over, took the reins from Jane, and mounted Dark Horse. Jane held the gate for him, and he rode into the pasture where Howie was moving around, and then Jane closed the gate. She put her boot up on the bottom pipe, leaned over the top rail, and relaxed, as if expecting this to take a while. Wiley started walking his horse around the pasture, as Howie ran in spurts, snorted, and threatened, but Wiley and Dark Horse just kept walking, turning, and circling. Howie was getting curious and started following them at a distance.

When Wiley turned his horse toward Howie, she ran. Sometimes, she would run parallel to him, then suddenly cut in front of Wiley, as if trying to get Dark Horse to follow her and give up this bossy human who held him captive, but the old gelding stayed calm. At one point, Howie seemed to be putting on her own bronc show, running around the pasture at full speed, kicking, and whirling, and occasionally trumpeting, which was a sound mares don't often make—unless they think they're in charge or in distress. These antics went on for half an hour, until sweat was dripping off horses and humans, including those of us just watching.

Finally Wiley maneuvered Dark Horse to the outside of Howie, moving her along the pipe-rail fence beside him, without touching her or crowding her. She seemed to feel comforted, having the black gelding beside her. After a few trips around the pasture, he slowed and walked. She walked. And then as deftly as I'd ever seen anyone move, Wiley leaned over and snapped a lead rope onto her halter's tie ring, then wrapped the end of the lead around his saddle horn. Howie obviously realized she'd been caught, and she bucked and yanked, but Wiley sat back in the saddle, and Dark Horse just dug his feet in and stood still.

Jane was moving in his direction. "Long as you got her, let's stall her."

Cal ran to the barn, opened a stall from the back side, and swung open the gate to the pipe run. It took a few starts, and stops, and whirls, but Wiley got Howie into the run, and Cal slammed the gate closed. From there Howie could race up and down in a 20 x 30 run that led to a stall.

"That was the nicest bit of cowboy work I've seen in a while." Cal whistled appreciatively. Wiley seemed pleased to hear it and tipped his hat.

"Whatever you do now, don't let her loose until we tell you. We need to evaluate her," Wiley ordered. He dismounted and led Dark Horse over to the stall-run, then let him hang his head over the rail and nicker to Howie, who acted as if he was a traitor for bringing her in. But after about fifteen minutes, she moved past Dark Horse and, just for an instant, touched her nose to his and blew her breath into him.

Jane chuckled. "Well now, seems like the high-strung mare likes the calm, quiet type." She glanced at me and smiled, making me blush. No way was I ever getting involved with someone like Jane Barrow, but her playful energy awakened me again and made what was already a hot day much hotter.

"I'm thinkin' about working with the mare at night," she said. "Cooler, and fewer distractions. Will that bother you, if I'm over here late?"

"That's fine. I'll give you a gate code." I shrugged.

"Appreciate it," she replied and got back into her SUV, waiting for Wiley to load Dark Horse, and then they were gone. I found myself not liking it when she left and just waiting for her to return.

❖

The following day, Cal asked me to come down to the arena and serve as a surrogate judge as she rehearsed a couple of riders for an upcoming competition. The aisles were awash in little girls dragging their ponies around. Along the tack aisle, they polished their saddles, and in the outdoor arena, a few practiced their riding skills. The older girls had the big indoor arena today, and Carolyne Remington, Sara Belle Windom, and two other girls were all on horseback in the ring, warming up. Ellie was on horseback too, in case anyone needed immediate help and because Ellie enjoyed a break from being "barn help" and liked getting a few pointers from Cal. Mrs. Remington and a woman I didn't recognize stood at the rail chatting and watching her daughter Carolyne.

"Let's circle on the left rein, at a walk, please." Cal gave the riders a few minutes to collect their horses and begin to move out as she turned on the music in the arena, a nice instrumental with rhythm changes. "Now a working jog, please." The five horses trotted. "Let's lope our horses." And they moved into a nice, cowgirl, rocking-horse lope. "Now reverse directions, right shoulder to the rail." She had them repeat the moves, warming the horses up equally on both sides. "Now, I'll count you down for the lead changes. Here we go, on the right lead. On the count of four you'll change to the left lead. One, and two, and three, and change." She gave everyone time to get their horses on the left lead. "Now one, and two, and three, and change. You should be on your right lead." The lead changes were a bit messy, with the exception of Ellie and Carolyne Remington, who had mastered the work. "Okay, walk. Loose rein, relax your body, and relax your horse. And halt."

"Making progress!" I said to the girls, who beamed back. "Nice job, Carolyne."

Mrs. Windom appeared on my left, startling me, always seeming to materialize like an apparition. "She's having trouble, isn't she?" She referenced Sara Belle, who looked despondent.

"Everyone learns at her own pace," I said, nonchalantly.

"I ran into a woman who teaches Olympic riders. She wants to work with Sara Belle," she said. The only reason for an Olympic-level trainer to work with Sara Belle was for Olympic-sized bucks, I thought, but then maybe I was jaded. Mrs. Windom moved in closer and made sure her arm rested next to mine. "You're the only reason I've delayed. I think you could provide what I need…for Sara Belle."

Cal came to my rescue, greeting Mrs. Windom and complimenting Sara Belle's improvement, which frankly I thought was a stretch. She still didn't have a good seat, and her riding britches were packed like a suitcase bound for Europe.

She was smart enough to realize her current style of equestrian clothing didn't fit her form and, by age forty, would no doubt be paying a therapist to figure out why she had anxiety about her appearance. Cal's arrival gave me reason to extricate myself, saying I needed to go over and talk to the vet. That was partially true. I needed to go talk to anybody whenever Margaret Windom was around. Mrs. Windom reminded me of a calico barn cat, always plotting her next pounce.

Chapter Seven

A vet truck I'd never seen was parked over by Howie's pipe run, and Jane was talking to a craggy old horse doc I'd never met. Spotting me, she waved me over and introduced me, saying he came highly recommended for horses like Howie.

"Which means," he grinned, "I'm dumb enough to get into a small enclosure with difficult women." He glanced at Jane. "Can't get her in the vein, so let's Ace her and see how that works."

He got the injectable sedative ready, while Jane dropped down inside the pipe enclosure and picked up the lead rope that Wiley had left hanging from Howie's halter—not the usual practice to leave halter ropes hanging off horses, but this was not the usual horse. Howie showed the whites of her eyes and pulled away, trying to take off and drag Jane with her. Jane cannonballed to the ground, becoming a dead weight, a human anchor that prevented Howie from whipping her around. When Howie stopped pulling, Jane bounced back up.

"Watch yourself," the vet ordered and then slapped a shot into Howie's neck, like he was darting a raging bull. It didn't look like it went as smoothly as he'd hoped. Nonetheless, he got the meds in and the needle out before Howie could trample them both. He climbed up over the rails, but Jane stayed down with Howie, who, within minutes, was looking sleepy and like she didn't know what had happened. Her eyes were drooping, her head falling down to her knees, and her body swaying as if she might fall over. Jane wedged her back up against Howie's shoulder and held her head up, talking in a kind, low voice to the horse, explaining everything was going to be all right. I wanted her to hold me and tell me the same thing.

The old vet opened his giant silver toolbox and brought out a pair of mouth clamps. He slung a rope up over the top bar of the stall and used it to hoist Howie's head up and keep it there. Then he put the clamps in Howie's mouth and cranked her mouth open to examine her teeth, perhaps thinking she had an abscess or teeth shards that would cause her pain and explain her temperament. "Young horse," he said. "Mouth's in pretty good shape." He took the clamp off and used his stethoscope to listen to her heart and lungs. He ran his hands over her backbone and hips, then put a thermometer up her rectum to get a temp, and finally took a fecal specimen and drew blood. Last, he shined a light in her eyes, looking for abnormalities, and finally backed away, saying, "Don't know how she ended up in a kill pen, aside from her personality. I'd say she needs socializing."

"You think they gave her any shots or wormer?" Jane asked me.

"Cal has paperwork that says she got her shots, but I don't know how they got them in her, unless by drone."

"I'll put wormer in her feed. Can't do any Ivermectin while she's semiconscious, and when she's not, I don't want to stick anything down her throat just yet. You bill me?" she said to the vet, and he said he would, then drove off.

Jane was still in the pen with Howie, stroking her and talking to her. "I think you're probably a good horse who's just pissed off. You might have done what you thought was expected of you, and then someone didn't think that was good enough, and they did this to you. Well, things are going to get better. Let's have a look at your feet." Jane let go of Howie's head and turned to face her rear. She leaned her entire body against Howie's left shoulder, then ran her hand down the horse's leg to the hoof and picked it up off the ground with some difficulty. She put it down quickly, as the sedated horse was having a hard time not falling over. "Think we'll save this for another time," she said to Howie, and patted her on the butt.

When the mare started to come around, Jane kept the horse's head pressed to her chest, as if imprinting her scent on the animal. After an hour the horse was awake enough to chew without choking, and Jane took a horse cookie out of her pocket and fed her. Then another. And then Jane leaned back against the pipe rail and just let the animal get used to her being in the run with her. After a while, Jane walked past the horse and out through the gate, and Howie watched her go out of the corner of her eye. I watched her go too. The woman had charisma. Even a difficult mare knew that.

❖

Jane kept coming over to see Howie, but most of the time to sit on the top rail of the run-pipe and just watch her, and coax her over for a treat or a head-pat. The horse had plenty of grain and hay, and was starting to put on a little weight. One evening, I walked over to watch Jane and Howie, and Jane beckoned when she caught sight of me. I thought she wanted company, but it was a business transaction. She had a check for three hundred dollars and a single sheet of handwritten paper that said I was transferring ownership of Howie to her, with her promise that she would treat her well, and if she ever had to sell her, the horse could revert back to me for three hundred dollars. I demurred, but she insisted, so I signed the paper.

"You do this a lot? Win ranches in poker games and buy crazy horses on a whim?"

"Now does this horse look crazy to you? She knows this ranch on the north is for show ponies, and the ranch on the south is for working stock. She's a working girl." She reached over and patted Howie, who pressed into her hand. I reached over to pet her too, and Howie flipped her butt to me, reminding me of Mrs. Windom, except in the horse world, turning a butt to someone is a sign of disrespect and wanting no part of you.

Jane laughed. "She gave you the hoof."

"You like that, don't you, that the damned horse has already fallen for you?" I realized I'd used the word fallen when I should have said "taken a liking to you," or something less personal, but it was too late, and Jane couldn't resist the entre.

"Lot of mares fall for me, because I take the time to get to know them, take good care of them, bring them dinner under the moonlight, put up with their smart-aleck, butt-flipping ways, and then one day, I win them over." She gave me a grin, and I looked away. "Gonna be that way with Howie. You have a good night." And she slipped down off the railing and walked to her SUV.

She's toying with me again, because she knows she's charismatic. She's probably had a woman every time she competes in an event. I'm spending too much time hanging out with her anyway.

❖

For a week I made it a point to stay away from Jane Barrow, but Cal seemed to be available any time Jane brought Wiley along. He would stay and chat, long after Jane headed back to her ranch, and sometimes Cal gave him a ride back.

"You and Wiley have kind of hit it off, looks like," I said, when she came back from having dropped him off one afternoon.

"He's a nice guy. Not my type, but a nice enough guy," she said, as she fidgeted and twirled, playing with her hair like a teenager.

"Hmm. Don't mean to pry, but why exactly is he not your type?"

"Cowboy. They can't hold down a job, spend all their money rodeoing, and sleep with every girl on the circuit," she said, already angry for his presumed infidelity, when they weren't even paired off.

"Well, good that you figured that out," I said, then fretted over what would happen if Cal ever did fall for someone and moved away to be with him. I'd be screwed. No one to run the school and teach the kids. *I better start looking for a backup now.* What was I thinking? No way to run a business. I didn't even have a money partner I could lean on or a business partner with whom I could strategize. The idea that one small issue, like Cal falling in love and leaving, could tank me made me sweat and worry.

That night I tossed in bed. I'd been so preoccupied with my breakup that I hadn't tended to business, and that was unacceptable. I jumped up and paced, something I did in the middle of the night when I was freaked over a problem that had no immediate solution. Grabbing a Coke from the fridge, I walked through the big double doors that led to the office and punched buttons to avoid setting off the alarm—which would shut down the phones, which would make some worried alarm-guy ring and demand my secret code, and then I'd have to explain to him that I was just roaming around the house in the middle of the night, which was the most embarrassing part.

I looked out the office windows and saw Jane walking Howie in the pasture in the dark, pausing here and there to let her nibble the remaining green grass around the trees. It had only been a week, but Howie was looking less freaked out. Jane unhooked her lead rope and let her loose. After a while, she walked back to Howie, and the mare started to move away. Jane moved away from her and turned her shoulder to leave. The horse came up behind her, not wanting to be left without a herd, namely her human, and Jane led her back to her stall run. Once in her run, Jane began lifting her feet to check out the condition of her hooves. The horse let her do it, as if familiar with this activity. Jane gave her a big pat and a cookie. The way things were going, I could be in danger of losing the bet.

At dawn I requested a meeting with Cal once she finished with the students. I laid my dilemma on the line in a straightforward fashion. Without her, I'd have no school, and without the school, no income, and therefore, I needed a backup plan.

"Well, if you ran off with Jane Barrow and sold the ranch, I'd have no school to run, and I couldn't support myself. So aren't we just freaking about nothing? What would a backup look like? I mean, no one is going to understudy a riding instructor."

"Why did you say if I ran off with Jane Barrow?"

"No reason. It was just an example." She tried to look innocent, but I knew her too well. "I do notice how you kind of radiate around her."

"What does that mean?" I said, irritably, as if she was trying to change the subject.

"You know what I mean. Vibrate, glow, whatever."

"I thought we were talking about you and Wiley."

"I'm not leaving." She snorted and left.

❖

It was almost three weeks to the day since Howie had come to the ranch. The farrier was here early, and I wondered why. Then I saw Jane and Howie standing there—Howie was just as calm as you please—as the farrier worked on the mare's feet, trimming them and fitting her with metal shoes. Jane leaned up against a stall and watched, and Howie kept an eye on her, like she thought as long as Jane was there, she was safe.

As the farrier swept up, Jane led Howie over to the hitching post out back of the barn. I followed, staying out of her way. Hairy and Sally joined the farrier and began scarfing down the horse-hoof trimmings, which always gave Hairy gastrointestinal issues. I shouted at him, but it was a delicacy he would not be denied.

"That is such a disgusting habit," I said to the munching dog.

"Won't hurt 'em. And less for me to sweep up." The farrier took up for him, then shouted a good-bye to Jane.

She waved from her SUV, where she was pulling out an old western saddle and blanket from the vehicle, and she carried them over to the hitching post. Since Howie was newly shod, I felt she shouldn't be ridden for a day—kind of like putting on a brand-new pair of shoes and going to a dance—you'd be asking for sore feet. But I was sure Jane knew all that, and Howie was her horse now, so I stayed out of it.

Jane swung the saddle over the hitching post right in front of Howie, who startled for a second. She took a brush out of her back pocket and began rubbing the flat side of it over Howie before flipping it over and brushing her with the bristles. Howie seemed to enjoy it. After Howie had sniffed the blanket and saddle, Jane put the blanket over the mare, and when she got no reaction, she let her sniff the saddle and then placed it on Howie's back.

She stopped to pat Howie and gave her a cookie. Then she reached under the mare, pulled the girth under her belly, and loosely cinched her up. She glanced up at me in the doorway.

"This horse has done this before," she said. "Someone has ridden her, because the gear isn't spooking her. So the question is mental soundness. Can she get her head on straight so you can ride her?"

"How are you going to determine that?"

"Ride her," she said, and grinned. I wanted to say I didn't think a fifty-year-old woman should ride a horse that no one knew was mentally sound, but I remained silent. "I can see you have something to say about that, but you're holding back." She was responding to some vibe I was apparently giving off.

"I just don't want you to get hurt, simply to win a bet. Maybe Wiley should ride her."

"I don't think Cal would like that. Think she's taken a shine to him."

There it was again. A warning that Cal could hook up with Wiley, and run off somewhere with him, and leave me high and dry. Jane seemed to be able to read my mind. "Worry doesn't stop anything. Just brings it to you. And when something leaves, something better comes along." *Of course she feels that way, since she's probably left more people than Eva Peron. And she probably thinks she's doing them a favor, making room for something better.* Although truthfully, I couldn't imagine anything better than Jane Barrow.

Jane had a bridle over her arm, and she slid the halter down around Howie's neck, leaving her tethered to the hitching post, then slipped the bridle on her and put the bit in her mouth. "Not a bad fit," she said to the horse, then adjusted the nose band to let it fall a little farther south. She unbuckled the halter, letting it fall to the ground, and led Howie around like a puppy on a string wearing her bridle and saddle. Then she tightened the girth up again real snug, put the reins up over the horse's head, and walked her around some more. Finally she unsaddled her and put all the gear back in her SUV, brushed Howie down, gave her fresh hay, and put her back in her run.

"Rae, if you don't mind, tell Ellie we'll quit messing up this stall in a day or two. I'm just going to keep her here overnight, because tomorrow I'm going to ride her." Jane gave me a big grin. "Say around eleven in the morning?" Jane patted Howie and left.

Chapter Eight

Ten thirty the next morning, Wiley and Jane were currying Howie and tacking her up. Cal, Ellie, and I were front and center for this moment when the horse from hell was going to become a gentle riding mount for Jane. The butterflies in my belly were crash-landing nonstop into the wall of my stomach, and I didn't know why I was so excited, nervous, and fearful all at once.

Howie didn't look as placid as she had the evening before. She was a little jumpier and not entirely cooperative; at least she didn't look happy enough that I'd want to mount her. When Wiley cinched her up, she danced sideways, and he danced alongside her, to avoid being stepped on.

Wiley finally walked her to the arena, with Jane at his side, and stayed on the ground with Howie, leading her around the railing and letting her get used to everything indoors. She was on high alert—ears up, eyes open so wide they looked like poached eggs, and her forward motion, if you could call it that, reminded me of a high-strung racehorse being forced into the starting gate when she didn't want to go. In addition to the dancing, she was swinging her head and glancing up above her as if she'd been led into a bat cave, and at any moment, something could swoop down and get her. After a full three-sixty around the arena, Wiley stopped near us.

"Want me to ride her first," he asked Jane.

"Now that wouldn't be fair, Wiley. The bet was I would ride her."

"Oh, yeah. Forgot about the bet." He looked down at the ground, clearly trying to avoid our witnessing his amusement.

"I'd rather call off the bet than have anyone get hurt," I said, and I meant it.

"I appreciate that." Jane was looking at me. "But then we'd never know." I wasn't quite sure what Jane thought we'd never know, but her tone seemed more personal than professional.

"Know what?" Cal asked, worry in her voice.

"If this horse is rideable, and if Jane can ride her," Wiley remarked. None of us said anything else. I guess we all realized this could end up being the true definition of where two fools met: an accomplished rider who had a lot to lose if she was injured, and a horse only one step away from the guillotine, if she injured her.

Wiley held the reins, and Jane went over to Howie and chatted her up for a moment. Then she went to her left side, put her left foot in the stirrup, and stood up as if she was about to throw her right leg over the saddle, but then lowered herself back to the ground instead. Howie didn't hold still but kept moving. Jane stood beside the horse and put one hand on the saddle horn and one on the cantle, then jumped up and down on the ground, as if she was going to mount but didn't. The horse wasn't crazy about that either, moving sideways and whirling ninety degrees. I kept my eyes on Jane, wondering how she remained so calm.

"Holy crap," Ellie whispered. "I wouldn't get on that horse."

"Which is why we're not Jane Barrow," Cal said, and I wondered what made her so confident about Jane's abilities.

This wasn't a cutting horse, after all. This was Howie, the horse from hell. A whole different deal.

Jane went back to her fake-mount several times until the horse calmed down. Finally, Jane took the reins in her left hand as Wiley held the horse's bridle. She stood up in the stirrup, slung her leg over, and sat back in the saddle. Cal, Ellie, and I were leaning in with every move, and I was pretty sure we were all barely breathing.

"Good to go?" Wiley asked, and Jane pushed her hat down tighter on her head, then nodded as if about to ride a bronc in a rodeo. Wiley let go of the bridle, and the horse stood still for a moment, as if evaluating how much freedom she had. Jane touched her heels to Howie, and Howie took off sideways, whipping left, then moving forward, then making a sharp right. Wiley leapt out of the way as the horse headed off in all directions around the ring, and Jane seemed more focused on steering than on keeping her seat. In fact, Howie's erratic behavior didn't seem to trouble her in the least.

Jane slowed her down, bringing her to a halt. Then without touching her side, Jane just flexed her thighs slightly, and the horse took off at a quick pace, then slowed and walked. The third time, Jane didn't even noticeably use her body to get her to go forward, apparently just her mind, and the horse moved out. This time when they stopped, Wiley approached calmly and held the bridle again while Jane dismounted. Cal, Ellie, and I applauded. We couldn't help ourselves.

"She's a real sensitive horse and moves out real quick," Jane said.

"Saw that. Oughta try her on cattle. Might have been used that way," Wiley replied.

Jane sauntered over to the three of us, with Howie's reins in hand and Howie trailing behind like she was already Jane's own personal riding horse, and we all walked back to the barn.

"So I would say I won that bet, Ms. Starr," Jane said casually, almost with disinterest.

My cheeks grew hot. "Yes. Apparently you did."

"Cal, you have that envelope with the winner's demands?" Jane asked, ignoring me while loosening Howie's girth as she spoke and unbuckling the mare's chin strap on her bridle.

Cal asked Jane to give her a second, and she crossed the aisle to the barn office, leaving me to stare at Jane, who glanced back at me with just a slight grin, as if she knew what was about to happen would get a rise out of me. Moments later, Cal came back bearing the envelope.

"You want to open it in public or private?" Jane asked me, obviously enjoying the drama.

"I'm fine with doing it here. Cal, open the envelope."

Cal tore the end of the sealed envelope and handed me the piece of paper with Jane's demands on it. I glanced down at what she'd written, amused and embarrassed.

"Yep, gotta pay up," Jane said solemnly, as if sorrowful about my dilemma.

"What does it say?" Ellie asked, and Cal took the slip of paper from me.

"It says—" Cal glanced at the paper and then laughed. I silenced her, grabbing the paper from her.

"It says, it's never going to happen," I said, staring Jane down.

"You never struck me as someone who'd welch on a bet." Jane furrowed her brow. "Does anyone here dispute the fact that we had a bet, fair and square, and that I won."

"Seems to me you did," Wiley said seriously.

"You did," Cal echoed, and shot Wiley an amused look. "It's better, Rae, that you just take your licking."

Wiley suppressed a grin, which suggested he too knew what was in the envelope.

"What did Jane win?" Ellie asked, confused and left out of the joke.

Jane looped my arm through hers. "If you could give us a minute, Rae needs to get over the loss she's experienced." Jane handed Howie's reins to Wiley and walked me to the barn office, closed the door, and pulled the blinds down.

"When you wrote this, you'd barely met me. And further, it's not going to happen. I'm not getting involved with gamblers, bronc busters, and wild women."

"No one asked you to get involved. I'm just asking you to keep your word and pay up on your bet," she said, and I stiffened. "But you have to relax and loosen up, if the kiss is going to be good, and I want a good kiss, because that was the bet, and I won it fair and square."

"You can kiss my derriere!" I laughed nervously over my dilemma.

"I'd be happy to do that too."

"There's no deadline on this." I began trying to wriggle out of it. "We didn't agree when or where the debt could be collected."

"That's true," Jane said. "But I think I'd like to collect now, so it's not hanging over both of us, you know, something you have to dread. Just get it over with." She moved into my space and looked down at me, then pulled me into her and put her lips on mine. As much as I wanted to be cold and perfunctory, when she kissed me, I was pretty done. Her kiss was hot, and longing, and amazing, and made me tremble.

"That was worth every moment I spent with Howie," she said, and she tried to kiss me again, but I pulled back. Jane didn't loosen her grip. "The bet said I get to kiss you. It didn't specify how many times." Then she kissed me again, and this time it was longer, and deeper, and I was damper. When she took her mouth from mine, she had to hold me up to keep me from passing out. "What did you want if you'd won?" Jane asked, her voice husky.

"For you to turn the music down."

Jane laughed. "Damn. I'm glad I won."

Then she opened the door and held it for me, and we walked back to Cal, Wiley, and Ellie, who were glued to the ground, waiting for us to return.

"Wiley, we'll be taking Howie back to our place now to work her with cattle. That okay with you, Rae?" I nodded. She turned her glistening eyes toward me and said, "Thanks, for everything, including paying off your debt." Then she touched those long, bedazzled fingers to the brim of her hat, loaded up Howie, and she and Wiley left.

I watched her go. Cal kept staring at me to the point that I finally said, "What?"

"Can she kiss?" I made a hand gesture designed to blow her off. "You sure look like she can," she said, and left me to pull myself together.

Jane Barrow could definitely kiss.

Chapter Nine

C al stopped by the office to tell me she'd signed up two more students for western dressage. We had only three horses who were proficient in dressage when being ridden by kids who weren't, so we'd have to schedule carefully and keep the horses sound. "And the two girls are women of color!" Cal beamed, happy to make our stable more diverse. "One is full-blood Cherokee and one is African American. Finally!"

It was hard in Oklahoma to find families with the means and desire to give their children riding lessons. The weekly cost could go on for years. It also required riding gear and, if not a horse, then the partial lease of a horse or the availability of a stable horse. Most young girls wanted their own, which meant having parents who could afford to buy the animal, plus pay monthly feed and boarding fees, along with lessons, show fees, event costs, vet bills, and wardrobe. So when you put all that in the Oklahoma blender, usually white moms and dads were the ones sending their daughters to ride. Landing two girls from more diverse backgrounds was exciting.

"Can't wait to get them started. Speaking of 'getting started,' how's Jane doing with Howie?" Cal asked, and I was pretty sure she was more interested in Wiley than in Jane Barrow, but she had a little matchmaker in her as well.

"I don't know," I said.

"We ought to go over and find out."

"Now don't start your *Hello Dolly* routine. I'm not interested in Jane Barrow."

"I think you are." When I got my back up, she quickly added, "I didn't say loved her, had the hots for her, were attracted to her, or wanted to date her. I just think you're interested in her. And who wouldn't be? She's spent years doing what she does. I bet she can tell wonderful stories and knows things about horses, and gear, and riding that we've never been exposed to. I just think she's interesting." I recognized Cal's patter as her way of planting a logical excuse in my mind as to why I wanted to see Jane Barrow. She knew me well enough to know that if I had to admit to being attracted to her, I wouldn't let myself go visit her.

"She is interesting," I said, and Cal jumped up and insisted we go over now, just to "check on the horse."

"Come on, let's go. She told us to stop by any time."

We pulled onto the Barrow Ranch, and I have to admit I was nervous, but my nerves turned to excitement when I saw her. Always color-coordinated—boots, belt buckle, hat, and that face. High cheekbones, big smile. She flashed it when we drove up.

"We came to see how Howie's doing," Cal boomed.

"You're just in time. Gonna take her into the arena over here and introduce her to the young steers. See what kind of cutting-horse material she is...just for the fun of it," Jane said, looking at me with those amazing eyes and speaking in a soft tone that sounded sexual to me. She always seemed to be saying one thing, but the light that danced in her eyes said she was thinking another. And how was I supposed to behave? I'd just had a very sexual kiss from Jane Barrow, albeit for nothing more than a bet I lost. And now, was I supposed to pretend that never happened and be the neighbor on the north? The best approach, I reasoned, was to stay focused on the purpose of our visit—to see how Howie was doing.

Wiley walked over with Howie already tacked up and brightened when he saw Cal, giving her a big greeting and tipping his hat. We all walked toward the arena, and Cal and I hung over the rail as Wiley and Jane went about their test for Howie.

This time Jane mounted Howie right away, as if they'd been riding together forever, and Howie was calm. Jane stayed outside the arena, waiting for Wiley to get things ready.

At the far end of the arena, half a dozen young steers were being kept bunched together by two young boys on horseback, who were the designated herd holders. Their job was to keep the steers from moving into the area where the cutting horse was at work.

Jane leaned down out of the saddle to talk to us, and I gazed at the drape of her arm holding the reins, the way she half slouched back in the saddle like she was as comfortable as someone in a rocking chair, and yet, when the horse shifted even slightly out of the position she'd designated, she made the correction almost unnoticeably with her leg. I was as happy as an eight-year-old watching a cowgirl TV series.

"The idea," Jane said, "is to see how the horse reacts. You don't want one that's calm, and wants to be their buddy, and walks through the herd like she thinks she's a cow. I'd rather have a horse that's either real scared or real aggressive. I've seen a horse so scared of a herd of cows that he almost went through a wall to get away from them, and he ended up being the best cutting horse ever."

Wiley shouted to the boys in the arena to get ready and keep the steers together. He swung the gate open, and Jane rode in on Howie, easing up to the cows to kind of give Howie a chance to look them over and make eye contact with them, because as Wiley said, a good cutting horse can draw a steer forward just by locking eyes with him.

As Jane rode toward the herd, encouraging Howie to move in on one, Howie didn't hesitate. She launched into attack mode and suddenly lunged forward, tearing into the midst of the steers and blowing cattle out in all directions. For a moment, we couldn't see anything but hooves in the air, fur flying, boys screaming, steers bucking and bawling, Howie whirling and whinnying, and Wiley doubled over in laughter. Jane rode to the opposite end of the arena, to get Howie away from the action, and then leaned over the pipe rail where I was watching. "Howie's a little aggressive," she said thoughtfully, and we both burst out laughing. I didn't want to acknowledge it, even to myself, but Jane Barrow on horseback was thrilling to watch. She looked effortless, like she was born to be there. Comfortable, reading her horse and whatever else was going on. No wonder she'd been a celebrity rider. I'd pay to go see her.

When Wiley came over, Cal asked him what the qualifications were for someone to be a herd holder. Wiley said it took a long time because the riders had to learn to read the cows as well as understand their role in the whole process. Cal said it looked like the kind of work on horseback that built confidence and agility, or it appeared to. I knew Cal was up to something, and I asked her what it was.

"I think Sara Belle ought to come over here and start working with Wiley, learn a little bit about how to keep the cows grouped together."

"Oh, my God, have you lost your mind? The girl can't walk straight. She'd be trampled and killed." I laughed.

"I just watched two young cowboys hit notes two octaves above high C and scatter across the arena like crabs on coke. I think Sara Belle could do as good as that." Cal defended her, and Wiley laughed.

"Her mother would plotz!" I said. "That's not the vision she has for Sara Belle."

"Maybe Sara Belle needs her own vision." Wiley chimed in. "I'll work with her if her mother signs something saying it's okay and agrees to no lawsuits if she gets cow-pressed." He beamed at Cal, and she beamed back, and I had an idea this was going to be their personal project.

"Perfect. Now Barrow's got my horse, and you're giving her one of my students. What next?" I asked, and Wiley chuckled.

"Never know what I'll be over there wanting next," Jane said slyly, and I saw Cal grinning at Wiley.

As we were leaving, Wiley suddenly announced that Jane was going to ride in a cutting-horse event, a one-time celebrity gig to raise money for abused kids.

"We should all go and support her." Wiley beamed.

"As long as we all keep our expectations low." Jane smiled.

"I'd love to see you in a cutting-horse event," I said, realizing that with every turn I was more and more attracted to this woman, who I had little in common with and didn't want to be involved with, who was too old for me, and too randy, as the old cowmen said. The kiss had screwed up everything in my head. So I needed to pretend that didn't happen and move on.

"Saturday afternoon in Fort Worth. Can you get away?" Wiley asked, and Cal said she'd reschedule her Saturday lessons and we'd be there.

Chapter Ten

It was a good four-hour drive, and the event began at five p.m. sharp. Wiley said Jane was leading off the evening and representing the charity, riding to encourage the audience to contribute. My stomach was already upside down as I thought about what I would wear. *Now that is completely ridiculous, thinking about what to wear to sit in the bleachers at an equestrian event.* I look good in blue, I thought. Sets my blue eyes ablaze. At seven a.m. I was still changing outfits. These jeans were too tight, those were too short for the boots, another pair had a stain, the belt didn't match the boots, the shirt wasn't starched enough. I was worn smooth just from getting dressed.

As Cal and I backed out of the drive, I glanced south, where all activity had ceased, because Wiley and Jane had left early to get to Fort Worth's big coliseum that hosted a lot of summer cutting-horse events. Cal was upbeat and happy to have skipped the Saturday lessons, even though that meant doubling up next week.

As we hit I-75 headed south, Cal mentioned that she'd let Sara Belle go with her to the Barrow ranch to watch Wiley training Howie on the cows. I suspected Cal wanted to watch Wiley.

"Did Mrs. Windom agree?"

"Sure did. She was happy Sara Belle was getting extra attention. I told her watching cowboys work would let her understand balance."

I arched an eyebrow. "Bit of a stretch, don't you think?"

"Just so happened one of the herders was a girl, and Sara Belle asked if she could learn to do that." Cal grinned.

"Oh boy. I can hear Margaret Windom now." I glanced at Cal, and we both laughed. I took a second look. "Lost a little weight, haven't you?"

"I don't think so." But she had, and she knew she had, and she knew I knew why. She was mooning over that damned Wiley Evers.

"Excited about seeing Jane perform?" She tossed back at me.

"I think it'll be a fun day," I said, but I was excited, and she knew I was excited, and she knew why. I was attracted to that damned Jane Barrow.

Heading down the highway, we were sure a wanton pair, wantin' what we probably would be better off without.

Two Starbucks later, we were in Fort Worth, pulling into the massive parking lot at the Will Rogers Coliseum. Ahead of us was a wall of parked horse trailers, although I didn't spot Jane's. She'd left passes for us at the window, so we picked those up and headed for our seats, which were right on the rail in the middle of the arena. It was Texas, so there were big boys, big sponsors, and big diamonds. Young women in sexy cowgirl-bunny suits served a trail of drinks in the private viewing boxes, and people in the stands paid for all kinds of memorabilia and drank two-fisted beers. Women in fancy cowgirl outfits paraded around greeting one another, and the men were decked out in Justins and jeans. Nearly everyone wore a shirt with a sponsorship logo or a ranch brand. Fancy trophy-rings and huge belt buckles sparkled under the big overhead lights, broadcasting their owners' wins and connections.

Next to the performance arena was a second arena for the lopers, young cowgirls and cowboys who live on ranches getting up at dawn to feed, bathe, medicate, and work the horses, and today that included warming them up for the competition. Without an hour of loping and figure eights, many of these horses could be too hot to effectively compete.

I knew a great cutting horse was playing a physical game of chess with the cow, figuring out what the cow's thinking, where he's going next, and beating him there. Therefore, the footing in both arenas was some of the deepest of any equestrian sport, because cutting horses put huge torque on their backsides as they slide, and the front end gets pummeled with twists and turns. A good cutting horse is fast and strong, and can turn or stop on a dime, many times doing both simultaneously.

The announcer spoke over the loud speaker and asked everyone to be seated, thanked the sponsors, and then said they had a special treat in store for us. "Dark Horse, one of the top ten winners in the cutting-horse world, in retirement at the Barrow ranch, will be ridden tonight by his owner, the legendary world champion Jane Barrow, a longtime advocate for abused kids. She's donating the proceeds from her appearance tonight to Protect Kids from Child Abuse. You too can donate by going to Protectthekids.com. And, as many of you know, Dark Horse was a slaughter rescue, which goes to show that a great horse is not necessarily the most expensive horse, but the one with the biggest heart."

"A rescue horse!" I said in dismay, and Cal grinned like she already knew that little tidbit.

As the announcer finished his remarks, cowboys were moving about a dozen five-hundred-pound steers into the arena, and the herd holders were bunching them up at one end. A short pause, and then the turn-back riders were in position at the edges, in case a cow escaped and needed to be rerouted. The announcer said, "And now, ladies and gentlemen, let's get this event kicked off with Jane Barrow on Dark Horse."

The lights dimmed, and applause filled the arena, along with stomping and shouts, as the gates opened at the opposite end, and Dark Horse trotted out. He was sleek and shiny, and his mane and tail had been washed and groomed. The saddle was a glitzy black leather with all kinds of flashy hardware on the fenders, stirrups, and bridle. And Jane Barrow sat on his back matching him in black and silver and more sequins than I thought existed on the planet. How could she still look so masculine in sequins?

She touched hand to hat, greeting the crowd, and patted Dark Horse on his neck. Then she sent him into the herd. He moved in without hesitation and cut deep, selecting a big steer way in the back and drawing him forward with minimal disturbance, the cows seeming to shift slightly away from the action to make room for Dark Horse. Jane looked relaxed, almost an extension of the animal, as she and her horse lured the steer away from the cluster of cattle.

Dark Horse was "face up" with the steer when the animal sensed he'd been seduced away from his buddies and tried to cut and run. Jane dropped her reins, signaling she was "committing," giving Dark Horse his head, and she would appear to be merely along for the ride as Dark Horse danced to the steer's every move. Now the steer tried to turn back with a twist and run, but Dark Horse had him. The steer blew left, then right, then whirled, but Dark Horse responded, eyes focused, executing sweeping moves, low to the left, low to the right, cutting and chasing, and Jane along with him, effortlessly glued to the horse. Finally Dark Horse pinned the steer where he couldn't move, daring him to run. Jane gave it a beat, the steer turned his head away, and Jane sank deep in the saddle, signaling Dark Horse to quit the cow, then picked up her reins. The crowd roared, she patted her horse, nodded to the fans, and circled the arena once by way of thank you, as the announcer reminded everyone about donating to the charity.

I'd held my breath, never taking my eyes off her. Her balance was magnificent, her presence like something out of a movie.

"Hell, I'd sleep with her," Cal teased, and applauded and whistled.

"Yeah, well, you probably could, from what I hear," I said.

Cal insisted we go back behind the arena and tell her what a great job she did.

When we found her, she had a gaggle of young women around her, asking her to sign their hats or T-shirts, but she had a group of men, as well, chatting her up. I didn't want to become a groupie, so I insisted we turn around, go back to our seats, and watch the competition. Jane caught sight of me and held up one finger, as if to ask me to wait, but I pretended I didn't see her signaling me and headed back to the stands.

The cutting events were structured by the age of the horse, not the age of the rider. Younger horses were less experienced, but perhaps nimbler, while more experienced horses were in great demand, particularly for riders who weren't as seasoned. Watching the horses move with such speed and skill made me wonder how long they could stay in the sport, which was obviously hard on their legs. Yet like all athletes, they seemed to relish competing.

About an hour into the contest, someone slid into the seat next to me. I turned, and Jane was there. She gave me a hug and asked if I was enjoying the event.

"You know that you and Dark Horse were spectacular," I whispered.

"This sport is all about the horse. Two and a half minutes of thrills on an animal who can spin on a dime and has a stronger instinct and intellect than a lot of human beings."

"Well, they don't do it alone." My tone was unexpectedly dreamy.

"Funny you should say that. Recently a horse lost his rider and just went ahead by himself and finished up with the steer. Crowd loved it."

We focused on the ring, and Jane gave me pointers about the sport as men performed. "They have to make two or three cuts, draw out two or three steers. One has to be cut deep from the middle, and the horse has to move him out with minimal disturbance to the herd. If there's noticeable disturbance, the animal is marked down." *Does Jane Barrow sense that she creates a noticeable disturbance in me every time she comes around, as if her footsteps, her voice, her breathing next to me are tied to my heart rate?*

"Second cut can be peeled from the edges. Fewer points, of course. Horse and rider have to get the steer clear of the herd. Then, I don't know if you noticed, but I dropped my reins"—*Of course I noticed. That was the sexiest damned part.*—"which is a signal that I've committed the horse to that cow. When the horse gets a drop on the cow, it's mostly up to him from then on. Now look at that." She indicated the horse and rider in the ring. "The horse quit the cow. See there. The cow was still facing the horse, didn't have all four feet on the ground, and the horse pulled off. Points deducted for that. Can't let the cow get back to the herd or let the horse use the back fence to turn a cow. And the judges grade for confidence when entering the herd, and how you and the horse look working together."

I tried to pay attention, but the hum of her voice, and her cologne, and her proximity to me blurred my concentration. "Splint boots in front," I said, trying to say something intelligent and referring to the leg wrap. "And skid boots to protect their fetlocks and pasterns. Their back legs have to take a beating on those slides."

Jane paused a moment, then changing direction as quickly as her horse, she said, "I was thinking I'll pull the trailer back with Dark Horse, give Wiley a break. You want to ride with me, and Cal could ride with Wiley? We could have something to eat on the road. I'd take you somewhere nice to eat here in Fort Worth, but I'd want a drink, and I don't drink and drive horse trailers, unless we were staying over. If we were staying over, I'd let Cal and Wiley drive Dark Horse back, and you and I could keep your truck and go back tomorrow."

Amused, I asked, "How long have you been thinking about this scenario that you just casually mentioned?"

"Ever since I kissed you."

"I think we'd better skip dinner and drive back home tonight."

"Okay, but you're riding with me." She said it like it had already been decided.

I could barely focus on the rest of the event, or what she was saying, or the people who kept coming up behind us to tap her on the shoulder and remind her that she knew them, or tell her they admired her, or just smile into her face. That would be pretty hard to take if you were partnered with her—a constant sea of adoration lasered in on your lover. *Well, I'm not going to be her lover, so that's not my problem.*

When I told Cal the plan, she was all atwitter, delighted with the arrangement. Wiley stopped by, and Jane casually announced that she thought she'd like to drive Dark Horse back and give Wiley a break. He was out of the loop and protested, saying he wasn't tired and didn't need a break, until Jane said maybe he should drive my truck and take Cal along, to talk about their plan for Sara Belle. Wiley got real interested then, saying he could definitely use the break.

Jane said she'd be back for me at the end of the show, and she took off. I drank an entire Coke and then went to the bathroom twice, not wanting to announce on the road that I needed to stop. I was so nervous, I was sweating. *If nothing's going to happen, other than a drive home, why am I freaking out?* I spotted her across the arena talking to two young girls who were obviously fans, and that irritated me.

Around nine p.m., Jane reappeared and asked if we were ready to head out. We walked over to the parked trailers, and Dark Horse was already loaded. Wiley was standing by to assure Jane that Dark Horse had hay, and water, and was loose-tied and ready to go. I handed him my truck keys, and Cal said she remembered where we'd parked. Jane unlocked her big SUV, and I climbed in as she told Wiley we'd see them back at the ranch. The interior of her Expedition was all tricked out in King Ranch cowboy "cush." I assumed since she drove to her various gigs, she'd sprung for the luxury model. I'd googled it: her Expedition was well over a hundred thousand dollars' worth of soft tufted seats and romantic mood lighting.

Jane slowly pulled the trailer onto the highway. "Good night." She smiled. "I heard they raised a hundred grand on their website over the last two hours." She navigated the truck and trailer down the road. I liked her profile in the dim light, so strong it was almost chiseled.

"What got you interested in child abuse?" I asked, knowing most people are interested in what happened to them.

"Well, this is kind of an awkward story right off the bat, but I guess I'd tell you later anyway. My mom died, and my dad raised me. They were rodeo people, and my dad was a bull rider. He did all right, made money on the circuit, but things were always tight. Anyway, one night he was riding a bull named Hot Heaven, and he went out the back door and got double-barreled, one hoof landed right in his head, and he was dead just like that. I was thirteen at the time."

"Were you there when it happened?"

"I was."

"I'm so sorry."

"My dad had a best friend on the circuit. Buddies, blood brothers, that kind of thing, and he took care of me. Until one night, he didn't. He raped me, and I got pregnant. Of course I didn't want a child, because I was a child. I ended up going to live with my grandmother, who raised us both until I was eighteen, and then I went back out on the circuit."

I couldn't even imagine Jane Barrow pregnant and fourteen.

"Some people call it an unwanted pregnancy, or teenage love, or whatever, but it's abuse—someone older, someone you look up to, taking advantage of their position of power. End of story. So I support this charity."

"Is he still living?" I asked, thinking if he was her dad's friend, he would probably be pretty elderly.

"No. And I never saw him after that."

I sat quietly for a moment, then finally just followed my instincts. "Can you drive with one hand and pull a horse trailer?" I asked.

She nodded.

I took her right hand in mine, and for some reason I felt older, and taller, and stronger than she was at this moment. Maybe Jane Barrow needed more than applause and random sex.

We drove for about thirty minutes in silence, just holding hands, the radio playing, and at one point, Garth Brooks was singing "Rodeo," and Jane and I sang along to it. She had a nice voice. I wanted us to stay like this forever, just going down the highway singing.

Finally she let go of my hand. "I've got to let loose for a minute because you're making me so hot." I put my hand on her thigh instead. About halfway home, she suddenly pulled the horse trailer off onto a rest area, clicked the door locks, unbuckled her seat belt, flipped the armrests up, unsnapped my seat belt, and then, faster than roping a calf, pulled me into her for the hottest necking session I'd ever experienced. Her mouth was on fire, her tongue so deep inside me, I could only envision what having her tongue in other places would feel like. I was wet from top to bottom, and with her mouth still on mine, she had her hand down my jeans, leaving no doubt about how much I was turned on by her. I managed to pull away and come up for air.

"No you don't," I panted. "You are way too good at this, which means you've done it a few times before, and I'm not going to be girl number 324."

"Not quite that many," she teased. "You want me. We both know that now."

"Everyone wants you, and that's your problem. You have everyone and no one." I was still panting. "You have to find 'the one,' Jane."

She let go of me and flung herself back into her seat, trying to slow her breathing. "You're a smart woman, Rae Starr. And now thanks to you, I need to be hosed off." We both laughed, and I cuddled up as close as I could get to her in tufted-leather bucket seats. She slid her long arm over and put her hand in the crotch of my jeans, and we rode that way in a state of longing.

When we pulled in to the Barrow Ranch, Wiley and Cal were waiting, so Cal could drive me back. Wiley pushed his hat back and adopted a serious tone. "You two do all right on the road? Saw you pulled off to the side, but figured if it was something serious, you'd phone me."

Jane fought a grin. "Or the fire department." She shot me a look that turned me red, and Wiley suppressed a giggle.

CHAPTER ELEVEN

I wasn't in my body half the time. I'd let Jane Barrow get into my head, into my pants, and nearly into my bed, when there was no way in hell I was having a relationship with a woman who went after women the way Dark Horse goes after steers—walking calmly into the herd, cutting one out to see if she can outmaneuver it, and then going on to the next. My mistake was the thermonuclear necking session. The woman should get a belt buckle for that.

Cal came bubbling around the corner, ebullient over her new students—how quickly they were learning and how enthusiastic they were. She ended her comments with the fact that Margaret Windom, Sara Belle's mother, was looking for me and loaded for bear. She turned to leave and passed Mrs. Windom in the process, who was puffed up like a big bird, her wings flapping and her breasts bulging like a Butterball turkey's.

"Are you aware that Cal has my Sara Belle next door, involved with cutting-horse people?" She spat out the words as if something very distasteful had lodged in her mouth. And for Mrs. Windom cutting-horse people were indeed distasteful. She envisioned her daughter elegantly astride a Lusitano stallion, performing brilliant dressage moves, not astride a quarter horse wrangling cows. The former was near aristocracy for Mrs. Windom; the latter was cowboying.

"Mrs. Windom, there comes a time when a young girl has to choose what excites her, what turns her on, and it appears that working south of us is keeping her interested."

"She would be more than interested right here if Cal were a better instructor." She had finally gotten mad enough to spew it out. This moment was always the fork in the road. If a child didn't excel at riding, then the parent blamed the school or the instructor. If the parent left the riding school without resolving that issue, then she bad-mouthed the ranch, or stable, which could hurt business. So we always tried to keep the parents supportive and engaged.

"I don't even know those people on the Barrow Ranch, and my daughter goes completely unsupervised to visit total strangers."

"She's never been unsupervised. Cal has always been with her, and Cal tells me you approved of Sara Belle's visit. Would you like to meet the people who own the Barrow Ranch?"

"Not particularly. Unless you think they would be interested in meeting me." She flapped her arms as if about to take off, and I envisioned her ego a cape of feathers that ruffled with the slightest breeze.

"Why don't I make a call, if you're going to be here for a minute," I said, and left Mrs. Windom to phone Cal in private and fill her in, asking if she could reach Wiley and check to see if, on the spur of the moment, I could bring Mrs. Windom over. Minutes later, Cal called back saying he would do it, and I gathered up Mrs. Windom and asked her to follow me over. We took separate cars, because I didn't want to be trapped inside one with her.

Wiley was waiting for us, and he was the master of charm, twisting Margaret Windom around his saddle horn.

He joked with her and gave her important information about working cutting horses, how it was a discipline close to the land and one of the oldest skills ever employed by ranchers as they separated their cattle to brand them or care for them. He complimented Sara Belle, while saying training slots were so few that, if Mrs. Windom didn't want her daughter involved, he completely understood and had a line of girls waiting. He explained what herd holders and turn-back riders do, and how important they are to eventers—the herd holders keeping the herd bunched together and out of the working area, and the turn-back riders on alert to reroute any cow that tries to escape to the back of the arena. Then he casually began playing up Jane Barrow—who she was and what she'd accomplished. On cue, Jane stepped out of the house, in black jeans and boots, and a red-and-black cowgirl shirt with black fringe, and she stood there looking like a Hollywood star waiting for the paparazzi. She greeted Mrs. Windom, who I could tell was charmed from the moment she met her, because her voice lost its edge.

By the time Mrs. Windom left, she seemed to feel like she'd jumped to the head of the line and gotten her daughter into training no one else got, which was kind of true. I felt bad about the over-embellishment of herd holders, but at the same time, I felt she'd asked for it, and maybe Sara Belle would have some peace for a few months. Wiley even managed to get Mrs. Windom to sign a release, in case Sara Belle had an accident. As she was signing, she thanked me for arranging the introductions and assured us all that she'd coordinate with Cal if she had issues or questions regarding the training.

When Cal shepherded her out to her car, I stared at Jane and Wiley. "You two scare me because all this comes too easy. It's like you have a grifter routine, but I don't think you're grifters." I thought honesty was the best policy.

Wiley giggled like a girl. "Oh my God, JB. She just called us grifters, after we helped her out!"

"She's not very trusting, Wile." Jane pushed the brim of her hat back. "Something in her background I've yet to suss out."

"Kinda hurts my feelings." Wiley feigned sadness and walked off.

"Want to sit down with me out here in the open, where you're perfectly safe, and have tea or something?" she asked.

I plopped down on the porch swing and put my feet up. I could tell by the way she was looking at me that she thought I was pretty. Her eyes softened when she looked into mine.

"To ease your mind, I've worked with a lot of kids, and their parents, and just regular adults. I know which ones are in it for the love of the sport and the horse, and which ones are in it to make themselves look good. Your Windom woman is the latter, of course. Her kid maybe has a chance to find a life with horses, but not unless we keep her mom's ego assuaged. So frankly, my griftering, as you call it, is to buy the kid some time. Otherwise the mother pulls her out of your barn and starts over, torturing her somewhere else."

"Sorry," I said softly about my accusations.

"What's your background? Can you ride, because I've never seen you on a horse."

I drew back as insulted as she'd been over my grifter comment. "Yes, I can ride!"

"So why don't you?" she asked, and I shrugged. She waited me out.

"My riding horse died. Major was twenty-four, and I had him for nine years. I did the unthinkable—bought him online, sight unseen and never having ridden him. It was his birthday, and he looked kind of sickly in the picture, but I bought him anyway and had him shipped to me."

Jane stayed quiet, and her silence made me go on. "He didn't like strangers much, or other horses, but he and I hit it off. He was so medieval looking. But he had the smoothest gaits, and he gave me confidence. Yet he was sickly from the time I got him.

"Anyway, I was in the middle of the breakup with Meg, and my life was crazy, and I didn't go check on him for a couple of days. I saw the other horses running and whinnying, but I thought horse flies were chasing them. When I drove down to the pasture, I could see his body lying in the field. When I ran to him, the coyotes had already gotten to him and eaten all the soft tissues—his eyes were gone and his belly hollowed out. My beautiful friend was just devoured. I can't get that image out of my head, and I can't forgive myself for not going to check on him, and I worry that he was attacked while he was dying. We buried him over on the south side of the ranch. There just won't ever be another horse like him."

Jane was quiet as I wiped the tears from my eyes, and then she gave me a sweet smile and took my hand. "You know what I think?" She paused. "I think you need another horse."

"That's all you can say after I poured my heart out?" I tried to make light of the emotion I'd revealed.

"No. I think you need a new lover too," she added, and I laughed. "You are, by the way, one beautiful woman." She said it with such conviction that I could almost believe she was sincere. At least I wanted to.

Wiley came striding over. "You still here socializing with grifters?"

I told him I was sorry about the comment, and he said he liked a woman who could apologize. I changed the subject. "What are you going to do with Sara Belle?"

"Cal says she can ride pretty good, just doesn't look real fancy on board. Thought I'd put her on horseback and start teaching her a few things about being a herd holder. We'll find out pretty quick if she catches on."

My mind flashed on Mrs. Windom coming to grips with her daughter's new riding routine. Things were just getting pretty tangled up around here.

"Meant to ask you," Jane said casually, "how'd you get the name Rae Starr?"

"My mother said when I was born, she couldn't give me much, except a name that would make people think I was famous."

"I like it. Makes you sound like a western movie star." She put both hands in the air and then separated them like she was unveiling a big marquee. "The incomparable Rae Starr in *Bronc Riding Women of the Wild West*."

The way she said it made me feel like a movie star. Jane had that way about her—making me feel like I was more than I knew. *Who does that for her?*

CHAPTER TWELVE

Jane Barrow came by the ranch to gather up the gear she'd used during her work with Howie—blankets, lead ropes, a crop, nothing that Wiley couldn't have picked up, but I had a feeling Jane was really coming over to see me. After leaving her out in the hot sun for forty-five minutes, I strolled over to see if I could help. Leaving her out in the sun wasn't very hospitable, but it might bake the cockiness out of her. She was a little too self-assured, like a cutting horse who thought she had the drop on me.

"You look spectacular today, Ms. Starr," she said in that quiet, smooth way she had. She stopped what she was doing and just leaned back against the pipe rails to unabashedly look me over. "You are simply too beautiful to be alone." Her comment made me blush. "But," she quickly added, "you are controlling and bossy, so you need someone who can let that roll off her back."

"I'm not going to stand here and be analyzed by a womanizing neighbor who reportedly, and I've had several reports, has had a lot of boots of different sizes under her bed. Are you bisexual or just promiscuous?"

"Good God, woman. Last time we met I was a grifter, and now I'm a womanizing, promiscuous bisexual!" She burst out laughing. "Most women can't handle you. You know that, don't you?"

Blood was rising up in my neck. "If this is your idea of sweet-talking, you need to go somewhere and take lessons, because you're making me mad," I said, and she chuckled.

"I apologize," she said, and we walked into the barn aisle to escape the heat. The overhead fans felt good. Jane leaned up against a stall and just kept staring at me.

"What is going on in that head of yours?" I asked. "Wait. You don't even need to tell me. I know what you're thinking. And you're always thinking about that, but it's not just in relationship to me. You just want to chase everything out there, simply to see if you can catch it, and of course you can, but once you have it, well, it doesn't fix that feeling you're trying to fix. So I think you should quit thinking what you're thinking and try to be friends first."

Jane just smiled and shook her head, and said nothing, which really wound me up. "You can grin all you want, but you know I'm right. I know who you are, and what you're thinking, and what you're up to, all the time."

"Are you through now?" she asked.

"I may not be. We'll see."

"You know, you're kind of like that mare I gentled. Constantly trying everyone's patience to see how much they love her."

"And do you love that kind of mare?" I asked, surprised by my soft tone.

"Always like to ride 'em first." She grinned, and something about that cocky remark just annoyed the hell out of me, so I kicked a feed bucket in her direction, and she stopped it with her foot like it was a soccer ball. "I'm going to come right to the point with you, because you seem to be a woman who appreciates straightforwardness. I want you, Rae Starr. Every time I see you, I want to tear your clothes off, throw you down, and make love to you all night. I'm just putting you on notice. I usually get what I want. So if you want to be left alone, now's your chance. You'd better stay away from me."

"You don't really know anything about me!"

"Even better. Pure lust." She gave me the Barrow grin.

"That's not on my agenda, so I'll do just that—stay away from you." I turned to leave all atwitter and unable to focus, as Jane echoed in the background, "Agenda?"

Just ahead walking toward me from the barn parking area, Megan appeared, my former lover who'd found someone she loved better and deserted me and the ranch a few years back. She had the audacity to be standing there teary-eyed, looking at me like a homeless puppy, as if she wanted to throw herself on me. I was sure that Jane was standing right behind us in the barn aisle, watching the entire drama.

"What are you doing here?" My question was that trite, polite thing everyone says instead of "Oh, fuck. Not you!"

Megan was about two inches taller than me, with dark hair and an interesting angular face that made her look like a lot of different cultures all blended into one. She could have been Italian or Polynesian or Hispanic, which is why most everyone thought she was one of them. Back East, people thought she was Greek. Here in Oklahoma, she got pegged as a pretty Native American. She used to dress in nice jeans and jackets, but her hippie paramour must have changed her style, because she was wearing loose pants and a striped serape that made her look like the love child of a Mexican maracas player and the clerk at Chico's.

"I came home to see my parents...and specifically to see you." She glanced at Jane as if to communicate that she still owned the ranch, which she didn't, and she was dismissing this interloper. She knelt down and hugged Hairy and Sally, who completely betrayed me by wagging their tails and licking her face and seeming happy to see her. "Well, somebody's glad to see me," she baby-talked to the dogs for my benefit.

Jane stepped forward and introduced herself, adding, "So you must be the former co-owner of Rae's ranch. I'll leave you two alone. Call me, Rae," she said, in an uncharacteristic plea, and she drove off.

"Who's that?" Megan asked.

"My neighbor," I replied.

"She has the hots for you," she said, looking in the direction of Jane's departure.

"Is that what you came to tell me? Why are you here?" I asked, but I could tell from her deflated body posture and the light in her eyes that she wanted to talk about what had happened with us. She asked if we could go inside, and I paused, thinking it wasn't a good idea, but she was already bounding up onto the porch.

Indoors, she began making herself at home, crossing the wood-paneled great room to the fridge, where she pulled out a Coke. "Glad to see you still keep me stocked up."

My hackles were up. How dare she wander around acting as if she owned the place when she didn't. Further, she'd left me with a big-assed mortgage, a struggling business, and a whole lot of anger about why she ran around on me with some sleazy little chick she was fucking behind my back. "Meg, this is my home now, not ours. What did you come here to tell me?"

"That I love you and want you back." She plunked her drink down on the marble countertop and made a move toward me, but I sidestepped her. "I think I had a midlife crisis—"

"And another woman," I quickly added. "What happened to Tonya? Is she here visiting your folks or back East practicing her shape-shifting?" It wasn't kind, but then Tonya did seem to have two personalities, and I wasn't fond of either one of them.

"She wasn't you," Meg said, and that remark just set me off.

"Now that is the all-time, most stupid-ass remark of the century! You had me, and you left me for someone who turned out not to be me? That just sounds like bullshit. Like you have no place to go, and no one to go there with, and so you're back here on my doorstep, but I can tell you, you're not, because I was through with you then, and I'm even more through with you now!" I ran out of air on that sentence and just came to a halt.

"Can I spend the night? You know how I hate Mom's place. And you could make me some of those buttermilk pancakes you always fixed for me—you could think of them as sympathy pancakes." Now she was acting like a little girl, which always irked me.

"I'm all out of the main ingredient...sympathy," I said, turning her around and pushing her out the front door as she tried a different tactic.

"You can't make it on your own, Rae. No offense, but you just aren't the business head. And you're so straightforward, you can't work the kids or their mothers. That was always me, smoothing things over. You need me and I need you."

"Meg, go home to your mom." I held her car door open, and she climbed in.

"Think about it overnight and call me." She drove off, tossing her long hair and pretending she'd won. I walked back inside, locked the door, and then went to the computer and deleted her personal gate code so she couldn't get in again.

Cal walked around the corner just as Meg was pulling away. I could see her through the window, hands on hips, staring after the vehicle Meg was driving. The minute Meg was out of sight, Cal dashed to the door and banged on it, quizzing me before I got the screen unlocked.

"Was that who I think it was?" she asked, and I nodded. "She's got some nerve. You didn't agree to anything with her, right? No lunch or dinner or whatever?"

"No whatever."

"Wiley just phoned to say he saw Jane comin' back to her ranch looking like a dog that had been kicked, and he asked her what was wrong, and she said Rae's ex-lover was back."

I didn't say a word. What was there to say? She was accurate. Meg was back.

"I'm just going to tell you this once, because I have to break a confidence to do it, but Wiley said, 'JB's pretty messed up over Rae.'"

"What the hell does 'messed up' mean?"

"Can't think, can't function, heartbroken, in love. Good God. Do I have to get a stone tablet and carve it out for you?"

"I've thought about it long and hard, Cal. She's so charismatic, I just don't think she knows how to be faithful. I mean, if Meg can't be faithful to me, why would I expect Jane Barrow to be?"

Cal didn't sling any clever rebuttals my way. She just nodded her head, as if she understood what was going through mine, and left.

Chapter Thirteen

Carolyne Remington's mother was a stately, conservative-looking woman who could have passed for a senator from Massachusetts. She never bypassed Cal to get to me, so I was surprised to hear her polite knock on my office door and to see her standing on the porch. I invited her in, wondering what could be on her mind. She apologized for taking up my time and said she wouldn't stay long. Then she thanked me for all the work I did for young women, particularly her daughter, Carolyne, who loved it here. Finally she got to the crux of her visit.

"May I ask that what I share with you will be completely between us?"

"May I share it with Cal?"

She paused. "No one else, please. I don't want a barn battle." She rolled her eyes, making me laugh. "Margaret Windom." She breathed out the words. "She approached me about having my daughter leave here and ride at another barn, and I think she's approached Rachel's mother as well."

"Why would she be trying to drive business away from my school? Is she unhappy?"

"I don't know. Maybe a friend owns the other barn, or maybe she's simply getting back at you for something."

"Any idea what that something might be?"

"She mentioned that you'd refused to work with her daughter yourself and wanted no contact with her, which she deemed haughty after 'all the money she spent here.'"

I let out a long sigh.

"I know. It's so petty and small, I almost decided not to tell you, but if it's hurting your business, I think you should know."

I thanked Mrs. Remington, who seemed not to need my gratitude. She was the kind of woman who had acted on principle and could now go about her own business, and she glided out the door.

A half hour later, Cal asked me to go over to Jane's place to watch Sara Belle working with Wiley. I was suspicious. It sounded like another matchmaking attempt to me, but Cal insisted it wasn't. Besides, I told Cal, I'd just learned that, despite Sara Belle's moving her lessons next door, Mrs. Windom was apparently hard at work trying to tank my business, and I shared the details of Mrs. Remington's visit.

"How long ago did Margaret Windom talk to Mrs. Remington? Maybe this all happened before we moved Sara Belle over to work with Wiley. Mrs. Windom could have settled down by now."

"Well, if she's hanging around here, pissing in the pond until no one can drink the water, you let me know," I said, employing a cowboy colloquialism.

"I will. Come on. Let's go check out our former student. I think you'll enjoy seeing her progress. It's nice when something works out," she said. "You need to celebrate things more."

"You Deepak Chopra now?" I cut my eyes at her.

When we pulled up to the arena, Sara Belle was on horseback, and she was happy, and she seemed to have a purpose—keeping those cows on the left side of the arena bunched up and calm, and she was doing it with alacrity. She still looked lumpy on horseback, but she could ride, and she had an energy and enthusiasm that made you like her. She was so focused she didn't even know we were there. Wiley was giving her pointers and shouting encouragement.

"He's so good with her," Cal said. She was obviously fascinated by him and doing that thing women do regarding men—judging them by whether they'd be a good father, despite the fact they didn't have a baby to nurture. Wiley took a break to come over and talk to us and signaled Sara Belle to join us.

She rode up alongside Wiley. "Belle's gonna make a hand. Doin' good!" Wiley said, and the young girl beamed. I noticed Wiley had changed her name, and it seemed to give her a more adult demeanor.

"Belle, you're doing great. Are you moving your lessons over here?" Cal asked.

"Yes, ma'am," she said, adopting the customary cowgirl politeness. "No offense, but I do think this is more me, and Wiley has a lot more he wants to teach me."

Cal and I broke into spontaneous applause and promised to stop over and check on her, to see how she was progressing. As we left, I whispered to Cal, "I admit it. That was a fairy-tale ending. She looks fantastic, and she's dropped a little weight and gained confidence." We high-fived. It dawned on me that I'd been hoping Jane was around, but she apparently wasn't, or she wasn't coming out to say hello.

As we headed for the truck, Cal surreptitiously tugged on my shirt. "Jane" was all she murmured and gestured over our shoulder. Then she took my keys from me, saying she had things to do for tomorrow's lessons, and if I needed a ride, call her, and she hurried away.

"You going to leave without so much as a hello or good-bye," Jane said, and she looked beautiful. She was wearing silver-gray sweats, the first time I'd seen her without her boots on. "Glass of wine?"

"If I stay, this isn't a signal that I'm agreeing to be thrown on the ground and made love to all night," I teased.

"I'm sorry to hear that," she said in a sultry tone that made me believe she meant it.

We sat down on the porch swing together, and she poured me a drink.

"So that was your former lover I ran into." Jane went right to the heart of what was on her mind, the same way I always did, and it dawned on me that we might be a little bit alike.

I nodded.

"And she wants you back. That was clear. Are you thinking about going back to her?"

"No," I said. *Is she just curious, or seriously worried about that prospect?* She turned her head to look at me directly, and I decided she was more than curious. For a moment, I thought I could see love there. "It's my own issue. I don't think I'm ready for another relationship with anyone."

"Your horse left you, your lover left you, and you don't trust that if we got together, I wouldn't leave you. Is that it?"

"I don't know if you'd leave me or not. In fact, I don't know if you even care about me in particular, or if you're merely competitive and don't want to lose to anyone, even my old ex-lover." I laughed.

"So you obviously don't believe in love at first sight." The way she said it made me think perhaps she did.

"With you, Jane Barrow, it might be lust at first sight. Anyway, I told you I'm not a gambler. I can't just give it a shot and trust that we'd be a winning combination forever."

"Meanwhile, there's this pesky issue about our attraction

for one another." She stared off in the direction of the pastures, and we were both silent for a while. "Where are the good old days when you just had great sex and decided later if you wanted to be together forever?" She poured herself more wine.

"Yes. I'm sure you miss those fuck-and-run days." I smirked. "Besides, how do I know I'm not just convenient? The lesbian next door."

Jane gave me a look that clearly said I should reconsider what I was saying. "So you believe I have to resort to the next-door neighbor for a date. Come to think of it, having a hot-looking lesbian rancher next door has allowed me to cancel my subscription to broncbustersdating.com."

A horn honked, and Sara Belle and Margaret Windom waved from their car as they backed out and headed home. I waved exuberantly in return. Margaret kept her eyes on us, and I could see her watching us from her rearview mirror as they drove away.

Once they were out of sight, I moved over on the swing, sitting close to Jane, who put her arm around me. I was sending off mixed messages, but I couldn't stop myself. I just wanted to be under her wing.

About that time, Margaret Windom came wheeling back up the drive, and I moved away from Jane as quickly and casually as possible, but I was sure she caught us sitting close. She leaned out the window and shouted, "Hope I'm not interrupting anything. Just forgot Sara Belle's new helmet in the barn."

Like Sara Belle needs that riding helmet tonight, in case the standing rib startles her and she falls off her dining-room chair. I was pretty sure Margaret had used the helmet as an excuse to come back to see what was going to happen with us after dark, and now she'd gotten her wish. She flew out of her Mercedes and disappeared for only a few seconds, and then she was back, turning the car slowly around and creeping past us as we sat on opposite ends of the swing.

"You two stay out of trouble." She beamed, and I knew Mrs. Windom had something on me. After all, this was Oklahoma, where piety was legislated and people were always eager to point out impropriety. Never mind that the most pious legislators, and clergy among them, were often caught molesting young boys in the parking lot, just before they confessed and found Jesus.

I sighed. How was I going to handle Mrs. Windom when she showed up at my office tomorrow? I turned back to Jane. "You were going to explain your many affairs."

"You force me to be far more reflective than I enjoy," she said. "When you lose your virginity against your will to an adult who should know better, it blurs sexual boundaries. Some women gain weight, become reclusive, and use their sheer size to keep men away. Others, like me, just figure what the hell, what am I saving myself for now, and for whom? So I slept with a few men that I dated in my teens, but that didn't work out for me emotionally. Then I discovered I liked women, and they seemed to like me, so after that I was a lesbian."

"Did you ever settle down with anyone?"

"I didn't have any place to settle because I was on the move all the time." She reached for her wineglass, and the loose gray sleeve on her right arm slid back, letting me catch a glimpse of an old injury. I took hold of her arm, forcing her to pause, and slid the sleeve back to her elbow, examining the long gouge.

"How did this happen?"

"That's an important lesson, right there. Got it bronc riding when I was in my twenties. I have another one on my hip from my one and only bull ride. My dad was crazy." Jane smiled, obviously thinking about him. "He thought it would be terrific if I were the only woman bull rider on the circuit. Never mind that bull riding is the most dangerous eight seconds of any sport there is. He couldn't see the danger for the hardware and the press coverage. The bronc scar I got in competition. The bull scar, just practicing at a bull ranch. After a few accidents, I started looking for an equestrian sport that didn't involve casts and stitches."

I rubbed her arm with my fingertips, taking this all in. "Back to the love affairs," I said, not allowing her to skip over her sexual history.

"Just a lot of different women. Longest relationship probably three years, but we never lived together, just hooked up between gigs."

"And what happened to her?"

"Kind of drifted apart, and she married some cowboy. What's with the ring?" she asked, suddenly focusing on the small diamond I wore on my right hand, having moved it over from my left after Meg took off. I decided, after we broke up, that the ring was too expensive to simply discard, and I couldn't see myself in line at the "we buy gold and diamonds" store.

"It's just a ring. Doesn't mean anything," I said.

"Then you should stop wearing it." She cut her eyes in my direction and I was pretty sure from her tone that she knew Meg had given it to me. "If the tree's dead, it's time to put up the ornaments." I wanted to say something clever in return, but she was right. I slipped the ring off my finger and tucked it into my shirt pocket.

"So you're looking for your next, maybe-three-year, relationship?"

She downed her wine. "Just looking for a little fun and excitement."

That wasn't the answer I'd hoped for but the one I figured

was most honest. Jane Barrow was excitement, and she didn't like contemplative moments on the back porch talking about memories. She wanted to go make some more. And despite maturing, she probably still wasn't very selective about who she made them with. Further, I'd removed my ring on her command and in return got nothing other than the statement that she wanted more fun in her life. Why had I taken the ring off so quickly? What was I hoping that would elicit? My behavior lately was unlike me, and I began obsessing over why I took the ring off. Suddenly, as if she could read my mind, Jane reached into my shirt pocket, her fingers brushing my breast, which caused me to lose my train of thought. She took the ring out and handed it to me. "Better put this in your jeans. I don't want to be responsible for your old lover's jewelry getting lost at the dry cleaners."

I tucked the ring into my jeans pocket. Apparently she didn't like the idea that another woman's ring was on my finger. And maybe seeing Meg appear back at the ranch like she owned the place had prompted her cavalier attitude about a relationship. Maybe Jane Barrow was just a tiny bit jealous. At least I wanted to think that.

"Want to go on a date?" She grinned at me. "Tomorrow night. I'll take you to the Indian casino, and we'll win some money. Good exercise for a non-gambler—loosen you up." It dawned on me that Jane and I had been to her events, and back and forth on the porch swing, but she'd never asked me out on a real date. "I'll pick you up around six p.m. tomorrow night." I hadn't agreed to go. The way Jane invited you was kind of like you'd already accepted.

We said our good-byes. Wiley came around the corner and insisted he'd drive me back, telling Jane he could see she'd been imbibing and didn't want her ending up in the pond. She laughed, and we left.

The distance to my ranch was short, so Wiley got serious real quick. "Rae, I'm just gonna say this once, and I could be wrong, but I've known her a long time. She's a heartbreaker. Not saying she's not all about you right now. Just saying be careful with your heart. Cal said you're a real straight-shootin' woman. Jane is too, just maybe a little less so in the love department."

I thanked him for the advice, but it made me sad. It was exactly what I thought was true, and I didn't want it to be.

Chapter Fourteen

The following evening, all the air had been sucked out of the prairie. While the cloud cover protected us from the sun, it acted like a blanket of hot water laid over a hundred vertical feet of intense heat, and the steam it created made it impossible to breathe. Ellie, Cal, and I checked on the horses and made sure they were in the shade. Beauty and Snow had put on some weight and were safely in their pasture. The boarding horses that were in the barn had their water fans turned on, spraying mist across them, along with cooling air.

I showered and looked for something to wear. It was hotter than blazes outside, one hundred degrees at five p.m., and the inside of the casino would be colder than a deep freeze. I finally selected white jeans, a white shirt, and a fringe vest I'd bought in Nashville. My leather belt and boots matched my vest, and I added a gold wrist-cuff in the shape of a horse. I ran my hands through my hair to loosen it up, looked in the mirror, and decided for the first time in a long while that I'd achieved hot. Jane apparently agreed, because when she pulled up in her SUV, walked up to the porch, and I opened the door, she whistled. Her reaction made me laugh.

"You're such a guy," I teased her, and she reddened, but when we went out to the truck, she opened the passenger door for me.

"Trying to live up to my guy-ness." She gave me the Barrow grin.

She looked spectacular. When she walked to her side of the SUV, I could see the back of her western shirt that lay across her broad shoulders, the piping coming down in a traditional cowboy yoke, the shirt nipped in at the waist. Her clothes have to have been custom-made.

I was happy. Just overwhelmingly happy. I wanted to be with her forever. *Now why am I thinking that? Forever for Jane Barrow is thirty-six months, shorter than a car loan.* She reached over and took my hand, and we didn't talk all the way to the casino.

She had a players club parking pass and pulled her SUV in underground. I hopped out quickly, not wanting her to get in the habit of opening doors for me. I didn't want to be anyone's little woman. If I'd wanted that, plenty of men in Oklahoma would sign up for the gig.

We took the elevator upstairs and stepped into a world of subdued lighting, flashing neon machines, clanging bells, and country music. Oklahoma had well over a hundred Indian gaming casinos, and it seemed every tribe from the Creeks and Cherokee, to the Osage and Choctaws, had their own gambling establishment, many replete with hotels, spas, fancy restaurants, and indoor theaters.

"I saw Ruth Pointer in a tribute to the Pointer Sisters here a couple of years ago. She was still sexy at seventy."

"So you *are* a gambler," she said. "Tell me what you'd like to play." I strolled past a monopoly machine with a wheel at the top that spun for jackpots and gave you the hope of winning half a million dollars, machines where you had to hit three horses to get ten free spins, machines with Chinese Dragons, and others with Cherries and some called Spinners that could lock up for hundreds of thousands of dollars. It was like a high-class carnival, and the bells ringing all around signaled winners. But there were losers too—other people shoveling money in as fast as the machine would eat it, then standing in line at the ATMs to withdraw from their bank accounts.

"I have to tell you the truth. I like to play machines that are pretty and the music or sound effects are exciting." I grinned at her, and she flashed me a smile in return.

"You're the kind of gambler a casino loves," she said, and I told her to go ahead and play something she'd normally pick. She selected a machine that went in increments from nine to a hundred and eighty, and it took me a few minutes to figure out the relationship between the increments and how much she was actually betting. One hundred and eighty seemed like it was fifty dollars a roll. She put a hundred-dollar bill in and began at eighteen, then twenty-seven, then fifty-four, then back to nine, then seventy-two, and on and on. Creeping up slowly, then dropping low, then going for one hundred and eighty. Pretty soon she'd racked up three thousand dollars, and I was impressed. A server came over and offered us a drink about the same time a dark-haired woman slung herself over Jane's shoulder.

"Barrow, what are you doing here?" she squealed, making Jane clearly uncomfortable. "You up and leave the state, everyone is asking where you went, and then someone says you won a ranch or something, and boom, you just moved."

"I did. What are you doing in Oklahoma?" Jane asked.

"Took a job here. Better pay and better opportunity, so maybe I'll see you down here."

Jane introduced me, referring to me as "her friend," and the woman shook my hand and then cut her eyes at Jane. "Well, I'm sure we'll run into each other again, and I'll tell everyone I saw you." She moved on, leaving Jane looking a little embarrassed.

"Lot of friends in New Mexico," I said. Before she could answer, a fellow appeared at her side shouting her name.

"I heard that woman say *Jane Barrow*! I first met you in Utah, and then I see you a few nights ago at the Fort Worth event, and now here you are! You're something. I've always wanted to tell you that. You got style, kid!" He shook her hand and walked off.

"This isn't turning out exactly as I planned it. We could eat in the club room here, but that could be dicey foodwise."

"Let's cash out and get out of here," I suggested, and we were back in her SUV in five minutes. "Where shall we go?"

"You know where I want to go," she said in that smooth way of hers, but I wasn't getting on the Barrow love-boat.

"Braum's?" I asked.

We pulled up to the drive-through, and I ordered a cappuccino yogurt cone, and she ordered a chocolate swirl. We parked, and turned the radio up, and ate every bit of our ice cream.

"I have an offer to do a round of clinics and lectures over the next thirty days," she said.

"Where?"

"Texas, New Mexico, and Arizona. Wiley will take care of things while I'm gone. I haven't said yes yet, so we'll see what happens."

I was distraught. How could she just up and leave for a month, but then why would she stay? Pretty tame here.

"Okay," I said, sitting frozen and forlorn. Then suddenly I was irritated. "Are you just baiting me to get me to give in to you? You always have an angle."

"No. I'm just trying to tell you what's going on, so I'm not springing it on you later."

"Yeah, well, it sounds to me like 'you better hurry up and get the candy before the store closes.' Sounds like baiting to me!" She looked dismayed, and I didn't give her time to counter. "You'd better think about what you're doing, Jane Barrow!"

I flung myself on her and kissed her until she couldn't breathe. I was putting every soft, hot part of me on or in her, and she seemed happily stunned. If there hadn't been so many overhead lights, Jane Barrow would have been in serious trouble, because I wanted her to remember what she was thinking about leaving. And just because I wasn't jumping into bed with her this instant didn't mean I wasn't going to... maybe.

"Take me home," I finally said when I thought I was dangerously close to dissolving in my own desire.

Jane looked like she'd been had. "Did that mean anything?" she asked, "Or was that just good-bye?"

"It means if I ever got involved with you, and you so much as looked at another woman, I'd hang you with your championship belt from the barn rafters. Just so we're clear." I panted. "And I'm serious."

"Oh, I believe you." Jane laughed.

One thing I knew, Jane Barrow was not the kind of woman to take subtle cues, so we needed to get straight about who was in the saddle. Jane Barrow needed managing.

We pulled into the RSR drive, and Jane hit the kids' lock, trapping me in the SUV.

"Not letting you go until I get an honest answer. Why are you keeping me at arm's length? Are you afraid of making love with me? You don't think you'd enjoy that or what?"

"I think we've kind of been doing that, haven't we?"

"We've been fooling around. Not that I don't love that. I just never get invited into your bedroom."

"Let's say we make love, and I become addicted to you, more than I am now, and suddenly I have to explain to little right-wing Christian moms, all the mothers of our students, why suddenly I've got this woman living with me, at least hanging on me, and giving me looks and…well, it's just a huge problem in this part of the world. Most of these people can't even separate same-sex-adult love relationships from heterosexual molestation of young kids. They think it's all the same thing, so if I kissed you, they'd think I must want to kiss their silly-ass little kid. It's disgusting, but it's a fact, and our relationship would become all about 'what will my students' parents think?'"

"And how am I different from your living here with Meg?"

"Meg and I had so little going on, people just looked at us as two friends, but you're different. You look different, and our relationship would be different."

"If you really believe that, then you can't ever have me, because you'd look like you're in love, and God forbid anyone sees that."

"I could only have you in big SUVs with dark windows," I teased, then flipped my seat back, and she crawled on top of me. I unhooked her belt buckle and yanked her belt off her, tossing it in the back seat, kicked off my boots, and unzipped her jeans. After I slid my hand inside and pressed my fingers against a soft wall of wetness, she moaned and shuddered, and thrust her hips into me, and came suddenly in a torrent. She yanked my bra up, took my breast in her hot mouth, and sucked it as she slid her fingers between my legs to return the favor, and I came almost before she could get there, having wanted her so badly. She held on to me, and we lay in crumpled silence in what would normally have been the most uncomfortable spot we could have selected.

"Jesus, I can never sell this SUV. I'm going to turn it into a shrine. Or maybe just take the seats out and install a queen-size bed." She was in me again, working me up, whispering in my ear, "I need you." It wasn't difficult to comply, because my wet, wanton body was making all the decisions for me. We were in the car for an hour, in as many positions as bucket seats would allow, before I said I needed to go into the house.

"Are there beds in there?" she teased, and I kissed her a long, slow kiss filled with desire.

I looked into her sultry eyes. "I love how you make me feel."

"I love you," she said.

How many women had she said that to? I wanted to be the only one, but of course that was crazy. If not that, I wanted to be the only one she'd ever say it to again. I gathered up my bra and boots and belt, as she asked if I was sure I needed to leave.

"Gotta leave," I said sadly, "or I never will."

Chapter Fifteen

I didn't sleep all night. And when I got up at two thirty a.m. and looked in the bathroom mirror, I appeared amazingly rested—cheeks pink and eyes glistening. I made coffee and watched the sun come up, wondering what Jane was doing, and if she was awake, and how she felt this morning. I wanted her to feel like she was in love.

At seven thirty, I was in my office doing paperwork when Ellie came over. Even though she was a kid, she was intuitive and always had the scoop on what was happening at the barn.

"Wow. You look terrific this morning," she said, and I thanked her. *She probably thinks I bought a new brand of makeup, because she certainly wouldn't imagine I'd been making love in a truck half the night.* "That Windom woman shouldn't even be over here, because Sara Belle's taking her lessons at the Barrow ranch from Wiley, but she's been here twice hanging over the arena rail and catching me for a chat whenever she can," Ellie said.

"What's she chatting about?"

Ellie squirmed a bit. "You. She's trying to get me to agree that it looks like you and Jane Barrow are real tight, and that you and Meg were lovers."

"What did you say to all that?" I asked, trying to sound casual.

"I told her I didn't get into that kind of stuff and acted like I had no clue. Want my personal opinion?" she asked, and I nodded. "I think the crazy old bat has the hots for you, but she's kind of like those horror movies where, if the crazy person can't have the woman she wants, she destroys her."

"Well, that's comforting!" I laughed, and Ellie grinned.

"Thought you should know, because she said she's coming by this morning to ask you to dinner. You could *be* dinner."

"Can you think of anything worse?"

"Definitely not!" Ellie scrunched her face up like a six-year-old who'd just heard how babies are made.

At nine thirty, Margaret Windom was in my office looking like the proverbial cat that ate the canary. She said she'd thought about me a lot, and with Meg gone, and no one living here, I must find it challenging, even lonely at times. "And now," she added, "people are shifting over to the Barrow ranch." I didn't bother to tell her that she was the only one shifting and that we'd facilitated the shift. I just let her go on. "So you must have a little more time now, and I'd like to have you over for dinner. After all, I'm no longer one of your students' mothers. I'm just Margaret."

"That's sweet of you, Margaret, but I have my mind on other things at the moment."

"I know," she said slyly. "I saw you the other night on the swing with Jane Barrow. She's quite a talented woman, but you have to be careful with women like that. I stumbled across these and thought you might be interested, although perhaps you already know." She pulled out printed copies of old internet stories about Jane Barrow. One was dated Denver, Co, June 1995, headline: *Barrow and Bevy of Women Arrested in Wild Night*. The next article was from a newspaper in Las Cruces, New Mexico, dated 1997, headlined *Woman Accuses Jane Barrow of Lewd Acts in Bar*.

I didn't take them from her or try to read the body copy. It was what I already suspected from the first time the farrier told me Jane had a reputation as a "rounder."

"Anyway, I'm glad she's not around any of the children, and I only trust Sara Belle over at her ranch because you vouched for her and Wiley is her instructor."

"I think celebrities on the circuit lead a much different life than you and I, plus these articles were from decades ago."

"I haven't looked for anything more recent, but you're right. I should. Meanwhile, I'll take a raincheck on dinner. Maybe we can do it when you're less tied up between ranches."

Margaret Windom sashayed her low-hanging, apple-shaped ass out of my office, and I wanted to throw a dart in it.

My phone rang, and an unmistakable alto voice said, "I just called on behalf of the Ford Motor Company to thank you for last night. My engine is running so much better now."

I laughed, in spite of myself. "Well, I wish your 'engine' could have been here a few minutes ago when Margaret Windom came to see me to share old newspaper headlines of you being arrested in hotels, and bars, with women who accused you of lewd acts."

"I'm sorry that happened."

"The fact that you did it or the fact that she has the proof?"

Jane chuckled. "Maybe I should have a talk with her. Belle's signed up to be a loper at the junior cutting-horse event. She'll exercise the performance horses and get paid for it, so I'm sure her mother will be there, and I'll say something to her."

"Like what?" The mere thought startled me.

"How about, 'Mrs. Windom, I wish your shaggy ass was getting laid by your husband so you could quit sniffing around my woman.'"

"I am not your woman! And don't say anything to her."

"My silence will cost you," she said playfully.

❖

The following day, we all drove to Stillwater to an arena near the university to watch the junior cutting-horse event for young riders and their horses. I'd agreed to go, on the spur of the moment, not because I cared about Belle's participation or the amateur sport, but simply to be with Jane.

In the loping ring adjacent to the performance ring, Belle was proudly warming up the horse of one of the teenage contestants. The big smile on her face and the jaunty angle of her hat said she was really enjoying her work. Cal snapped photos of her, as proud of her as a mom would be. Belle was her project, and it seemed to be going well. Despite that, I didn't see Cal smiling that much in general. It was more like she was just going through the motions and had something else on her mind.

Margaret Windom had already located Wiley and cut him out of our human herd, hitting him with a barrage of questions: Shouldn't Sara Belle hold her hands higher? She seems a bit slouchy, and posture should count in any discipline, shouldn't it? What is the next step up for her?

Wiley kept his bouncy attitude and big smile and said, "Mrs. Windom, Belle couldn't be doing better. I'm so proud of her!" Wiley knew the truncated name for her beloved daughter wouldn't sit well with Margaret Windom, which I knew was exactly why he'd slung it out there. Wiley was a good-natured needler.

Mrs. Windom followed up with questions about the young boys in the ring. "Are there any from families I would recognize?" she asked, obviously scouting for a suitor for Sara

Belle, and sussing out who among the skinny youths might have money or name recognition. Wiley played dumb, saying they were all upstanding, hardworking young men. I thought "all" was a bit of a stretch, but Mrs. Windom seemed to like it.

In between dealing with Mrs. Windom and Belle, Wiley kept craning his neck to get a look at Cal and trying to get her attention, but she ignored him as if she didn't know him. I watched the action for a while, at first believing that Cal didn't see him, but it didn't take long to figure out that she could see him, all right, but simply didn't want to. I leaned in to Cal and asked how things were going. "Looks like if it gets any colder between you and Wiley, he'll have to knock the icicles off his ass."

"He has a wife," she said, and I jumped back before I could contain myself. "Yeah. Small detail he forgot to mention." She gave me a steely smile.

"A wife, and he didn't tell you? Well, that's just shit on top of chicken shit." I snorted, feeling sorry for Cal.

"I told you that's why I don't trust cowboys."

I left the topic alone after that. Seemed like everything on the Barrow ranch was hot and sexy, and glitzy, and pre-owned. In fact, had multiple owners. The images of Margaret's internet search flashed across my mind.

Wiley tossed a look at Cal several times, but her expression was as impenetrable as the Great Wall of China—and it'd be a walk of about that distance for him to ever get around her again.

Jane stayed close to me under the pretext of telling me the details of the cutting-horse training for beginners, and I vibrated from just the smell of her cologne. In the arena, a young boy lost his balance and slid off his horse in the midst of heading a cow. The crowd moaned. "Took his eye off the cow and got dirt in his shirt," Jane explained. "The cow, not the horse, determines your timing and balance. Gotta keep your eyes locked on the cow."

My mind was abuzz. I loved being here with her and listening to her, but was I ignoring the signs—the internet articles, the way the woman in the casino alluded to how many people missed her, and frankly just how damned good she was at love making in tight places! The woman had experience.

"I didn't know Wiley was married," I said casually, and my remark caught Jane off guard.

"Yes, he is."

"So where's his wife?"

"I'll let Wiley tell you all that. I don't want to get it wrong," she said, and I recognized that as the cowboy code of ethics. Never gossip about anyone. Let them tell their own story. And frankly, I felt she was using that code of ethics as a big, fat smoke screen. *Jane Barrow can make love to me, but she can't tell me something about her ranch foreman's marital status when he's breaking Cal's heart?*

"Seems to me I don't need to hear it from Wiley, because he already 'got it wrong' when he failed to tell Cal he was married. And I don't imagine Wiley will be 'telling me all that' since he can't even find the courage to tell it to the woman he's romancing."

"You go off like a bottle rocket," she said.

"Really? You don't think this kind of betrayal is worth some fireworks?"

Jane didn't say anything, but I could see her mind clicking away. Most women probably wouldn't risk their relationship with her to tell her the truth. *Which is why she's alone and probably in some damned mess half the time. And she's probably evaluating me right now, deciding if my attitude toward infidelity will fit with her lifestyle much longer.*

When the event ended, I had no idea who won, nor did

I care. We headed back across the parking lot. Wiley walked with Belle, Cal shepherded Mrs. Windom, and Jane and I brought up the rear. Wiley kept looking over his shoulder at Cal.

"He's gonna break his neck if you don't look at him," I said with dark humor.

"I'd like him to break his damned neck," Cal muttered.

Wiley turned again, just for a second, to search for Cal, obviously sensing her hurt and anger and trying desperately to reconnect. Otherwise, he would have seen it coming and would have had the reflexes to save Belle. As it was, the event cart came wheeling around the corner of the arena into the parking lot and clipped Belle, flipping her backward. She hit her head on the cement and lay motionless. Mrs. Windom screamed far louder than Belle, and within seconds all six of us were on the ground with her, including the kid driving the golf cart.

Paramedics had been standing by for the riders, so we had immediate help. They lifted her onto a gurney and loaded her into the ambulance, and we followed her to the hospital. My mind contrasted the fabulous charity event where Jane had been the star and we had such a great time, with this amateur event that ended up with us all in the ER. Things had gone from good to bad in a heartbeat.

Once the examination revealed Belle had no concussion or internal bleeding, Mrs. Windom began searching for who to sue, starting with Wiley and the Barrow Ranch, saying they had put her daughter in this event. But since the event itself didn't injure Belle, Margaret Windom quickly targeted the arena facility and their golf-cart-driving staff. She informed all of us that her attorneys would see to it that Sara Belle was compensated for her pain and suffering, and future headaches. Mrs. Windom was her "future headache," as far as I could see.

Sara Belle was released after several hours. When the two

of them were safely on the road, we all headed back to the ranch. It had not been the best day. The thrill of love in the air had burned up like the prairie grass. Cal wanted to ride back with me and Jane, but Jane asked her as a favor to ride with Wiley, because she had some business to discuss with me. Cal was stuck and sauntered off, pissed at having to get in the truck with the guy who'd lied to her.

About ten minutes into the return trip, Jane said, "Rae, I don't want you to explode at what I'm about to say, so hear me out." She waited for me to whisper okay. "I'm taking that thirty-day-tour opportunity. Right now, this Mrs. Windom thing is heating up to the point that she could start affecting your clientele with her stories about me and how I'm involved with you. Second, I'm not good at hiding my feelings, and as much as I loved last night, I want a real home, with a real bed and a real lover waiting for me, and I don't want to have to hide that. I'm too old to play games with people. And third, I don't think you trust me, and I don't know if you'll ever trust me, and that's not a relationship."

I didn't say anything. Maybe this was Jane's way of letting go of me. She'd said I "go off like a bottle rocket." Maybe she thinks if I reacted that way about Wiley, I'd react ten times worse if it was something about her. *Well, she's got that right. I wouldn't put up with her flirting, or running around, or womanizing for one damned minute.* A stream of tears trickled down my cheeks. Jane tried to take my hand, but I pulled away. I didn't want to hold on to someone who was leaving anyway.

CHAPTER SIXTEEN

Wiley was at my office door before I'd barely had my coffee. He looked like he hadn't slept all night, and his eyes were red. I didn't want to see myself in a mirror, because I was afraid we might be a matched set. I hadn't slept all night and had cried half of it.

"You okay? You look like shit," I said. He was wearing scarred chaps, his boots were dirty, and his shirt was rumpled. He was nowhere near that spiffy, starched cowboy he always seemed to be. "If I didn't know better, I'd think you've been rolling in the cow pasture."

He plopped down in a chair and put his head in his hands, clearly trying to pull himself together. "Whole trip back, Cal beat the lips off me. She called me every name under the sun and then some. I tried to explain, but there was no explaining."

"Well, I'd say you had it comin', cowboy." I had absolutely no sympathy for his plight.

"I'm in love with Cal," he finally said. "I need your help, Rae."

"Help in choosing between adultery and polygamy?"

He looked up startled, and then started laughing. "You're a straight shooter, Rae. No wonder Jane's hooked on you."

I let his remark about Jane slide, but it did warm me to hear it. "You love your wife?"

"She's living with another guy in my house," he said.

"Well, what the hell, man? Now your two choices are to kick his ass out or divorce her."

"She's not right in the head. On drugs. Kind of psychotic. I've always just felt that if I divorced her, that might put her over the edge, you know, make her OD."

"So you enable her situation, even provide her with a live-in lover. You know, Wiley, sometimes the weak wrestle us to the ground. Their weakness is their strength. If you choose to let this go on, it means you're taking a pass on Cal, who's a phenomenal woman, but she won't put up with being somebody's honey on the side or being involved with a married man."

"I know," he said, and I let up. No need to grind the man into the ground. He already looked like dust the wind kicked up.

"How's Jane doing this morning?" I asked.

"Thinkin' about you, I imagine. She and Dark Horse left at four a.m. to start their tour."

I felt sick. *She left right away, this soon, without telling me? But then I guess she told me last night.*

"She'll pick up her team in Amarillo, which is their first clinic. She travels with two or three people to help with the trailering and the setup. She'll be fine."

I sat down in my office chair and must have looked stricken, because Wiley asked if I was all right. I told him I was fine, but I knew a man who could read horses could read me and know I was a far cry from fine.

"All that talk about her, a lot of it was jealousy," Wiley insisted. "She was always bigger than life, and it irked a lot of men, but it attracted a lot of women. I'm not saying it'd be any different if you were with her, but I will say I think you could trust her." *So Jane must have shared with Wiley my feelings about trust.*

"Now that's horse shit, because the other night you were telling me she wasn't the loyal type, and to be careful with my heart."

Wiley's teasing and needling gear kicked in. "Trust is a weird deal anyway," he said. "It just means you'll tell me what you're up to, and I'll tell you if it's okay, right?" He giggled for the first time in a while, and I always liked a man who could sometimes just giggle like a girl. "I mean, Jane could say I'm traveling with three women on this tour, and you could say, they'd all better be over sixty, and if she said they are, and they were, then you could trust her."

"Wiley Evers, are you telling me she's traveling with three women on this tour?"

"Now, I never said that." He giggled again.

"And none of them are old."

"Hauling horses, throwing hay, and setting up the ring are for young girls."

"Why would I ever trust her?"

"She didn't lie to you about it. You just never asked. Gotta be more inquisitive with JB, because she'll tell you if you ask, but if you don't, she won't offer."

It was true I hadn't asked. Why was he telling me this? Just to irritate me and make me jealous? Wiley picked up his hat off his lap, thanked me for the chat, and walked out the door.

I picked up my cell phone and dialed Jane. She answered immediately.

"So no good-bye," I said.

"Too painful," she answered cryptically.

"You okay?"

"Sure."

"You're talking in monosyllables because you have someone in the truck with you, maybe a woman?"

"Just picked up my crew in Amarillo." Her voice contained a smile.

"Your all-female crew?"

"Oh, boy. Is this what it'd be like?" she asked, obviously referring to what life with me would entail.

"If you were lucky enough that I gave a shit. How do I know nothing's going on with these women?"

"Here, ask them." She handed the phone to someone, and a woman said hi, then introduced herself as Sonny.

"I've heard a lot of good things about you, Rae," Sonny said. "Now when it comes to Jane, you can't trust her as far as you can throw her—"

I heard Jane cuss in the background, they scuffled for the phone, and Jane finally got it.

"She's just kidding." A pause. "I miss you already." In the background I could hear two women make swooning sounds, teasing her. "I gotta go. I'll call you," she said, and hung up. I sat there, wishing she was here and wondering when she'd return. Then, determined to shake those feelings off, I walked down to the arena, where Cal was giving a lesson to the pretty Native American student who was beginning her western-dressage training. She looked happy and comfortable in the saddle. When they finished the lesson, I applauded, and she ducked her head, shy but evidently pleased with herself. I waited for her to unsaddle, wash her horse off in the wash bay, scrape the water off him, and walk him out to the pasture, keeping my eye on Cal, who didn't have the usual bounce in her step.

"If there hadn't been that damned old poker game," I said, only half joking.

"What was Wiley doing over here?" she asked. "Lookin' to cry on your shoulder?"

"Crying over you. Says he's in love with you. Did he tell you about the circumstances with his wife?" I asked, and she rolled her eyes as if she thought it was all made up. The set of her jaw let me know conversation on that subject was over.

"Forgot to tell you, I got a call from this woman who's a mental-health person or something. Has these two old vets who want to come out and pet a horse." She rolled her eyes again. "Told her she had to talk to you." Cal pulled out her cell phone and sent the contact info to me. I walked back to my office and rang the woman.

Her name was Dusty Daniels, and she worked with older veterans who were depressed and didn't want to stay around. She'd discovered in talking to them that a couple of the men had once owned horses. She said she understood they couldn't ride, but did we have horses they could interact with? Their guardians would sign a release if I'd let them come out. I thought about Snow and Beauty, who weren't rideable and were basically pasture poodles. Finally I suggested Sunday might work for a visit, when we didn't have any riders here.

Late that night, I was curled up in bed staring at the TV, not really watching it, just kind of letting it wash over me like a blur of words and pictures that provided background noise for my mind's unrestful banging around. The phone rang, startling me, and when I picked it up, Jane's voice soothed me.

"If I were there right now, we'd be making love."

"You're awfully sure of yourself," I said.

"You'd be the one begging me for it."

She got the yelp of protest she was aiming for and laughed. "Listen to me, Rae. We've got to work this out. I love you. You've got to trust me on that. Yes, I'm flashy, but I can be loyal. I want to be loyal to you. So don't go putting anyone else in your bed, or your heart, while I'm gone."

"When are you coming back?" I whispered.

"You don't like phone sex?"

"I like sex in the flesh."

"I have three more events, and I'm done. And I'll be right there, wrapping myself around you and wearing your sexy little fanny out. I love you."

Jane had a way of talking that just hypnotized me. I didn't want to believe she really loved me that much, but deep down, I think I did.

"I love you too," I said. And I could tell from the way she took a deep breath, and the smile in her voice, that she was relieved.

"We'll figure all the church mothers out. Don't worry." After she hung up, my mind relaxed, and I slept.

❖

I didn't tell Cal I'd agreed to Dusty Daniels bringing some old vets out to the ranch. She had enough on her mind.

Sunday morning I walked the two mares up to the barn and stalled them, turning on the misting fans because it was already ninety-five degrees. Fifteen minutes later, an old beat-up Pontiac pulled into the drive, and a jolly, perspiring woman got out and gave me a big damp handshake, introducing herself as Dusty. Her wispy auburn hair blew in all directions, revealing patches of bald scalp—like she routinely ripped her hair out over her job at the VA.

The two guys in the back seat were slower to disembark. Dusty had told me in our phone conversation that they were both sixty-five, but they looked a lot older than that. Their scruffy gray facial hair prevented anyone from getting a good look at them. They wore baggy jeans, white T-shirts, and old, faded work shirts.

"Ms. Starr, this is Mike and John. Mike is air force and John is army."

"Thank you for your service," I said, in the way people are trained to greet veterans. "And please call me Rae."

They nodded haltingly.

Their faces were dull, almost slack, and their lack of enthusiasm made them look like they'd been loaded into the car to go to the dentist or someplace else that didn't matter. They walked haltingly to the barn. When they entered through the big double doors, Snow and Beauty hung their heads over the stall bars, and both men stopped and stared for several seconds. Then Mike looked at Dusty as if held captive and waiting for instructions.

"Can they pet them?" she asked.

"Absolutely. This one, with the gray speckles on her face, is Snow, and this one is Beauty. Mike and John, just take your time. These horses were scheduled to be slaughtered and turned into dog food, or human food. They were rescued and survived." I wanted to add "like you survived," but I didn't. "They're trying to recover, which is why they're so skinny."

Both men walked up to the horses and began to stroke their muzzles. We just stood and watched. It was amazing and beautiful. Finally Mike asked if he could go into the stall with Snow. I thought about the danger that might pose, but then I also thought it was a pretty safe bet nothing would happen. I slid the door back and let Mike walk in. He stood next to the tall mare, and then he began stroking her whole body, her neck and back, and sides and buttocks, and the mare relaxed. Mike looked happy. An hour went by before we knew it, and everyone hugged, and Mike and John seemed more alert. They thanked me and asked if they could come back. How could I say no? It required only an hour of my time, and it probably made their week.

Dusty took me aside as they were making their way to the car. She wanted to turn this into a test to see if vets, simply touching a big animal like these horses, became more manageable and happier throughout their week, as compared to their peers. She said if she could prove her point, she thought she could get a grant for a bigger program, and that would include compensating the ranch for horses and their care. I told her it sounded interesting but asked that we move off the Sunday schedule to an afternoon or early evening time. I didn't think it would interfere with our lessons, but I didn't want it to tie up my weekends, in case Jane returned.

I filled Cal in, and she looked surprised. "You fought me on taking in slaughter horses, and now you're creating a whole new business with veterans and rescue horses?"

"It was an accident," I said, somewhat apologetic.

She laughed. "Hey. I'm all for more old guys and fewer trophy moms."

❖

Over the next thirty days, we had six men from the veterans' home showing up once a week to work with Snow and Beauty. They led the horses around, brushed them, fed them hay, and mostly patted them. The horses reached the point that they nickered when they saw the men, and of course the guys loved that. What we were doing felt worthwhile, and it kept me busy while Jane was gone.

By the end of August, Wiley passed on information that Jane was extending her trip, heading up into Nevada. My calls with her were fewer and far between. Often when I reached her, I could hear loud music in the background, and laughter, like it was a casino, or bar, or rodeo. The background noise served to set my brain on fire again. *She wants me to trust her, but she's out every night. She says she's not calling me from her hotel room, because she doesn't get back there until too late to phone me, so she's finding places where she can place a call.* True, she was on Mountain Time, and I was on Central, but still—I had to work on keeping my mind from running away and making up stories about what she was up to.

❖

Mike was the one who noticed Snow was limping when he walked her. He touched her hoof, and it was hot where the hair meets the hoof, so we asked the vet to take a look. The old vet said the coffin bone beneath the hoof wall had probably separated out in the past, and now it was doing it again. If a condition like this persisted or got worse, Snow would have to be put down. Stress from multiple situations—a history of being mistreated and starved, and then recently the shock of the intense heat—had probably caused the condition.

Mike was so upset over the mare, Dusty worried about him the way we worried about the horse. We stalled Snow on thick shavings for now, giving her bute, which was the equivalent of horse aspirin, making sure no one fed her rich grain, and trimming her hooves to take the pressure off her rotated coffin bone. Once she was out of the stall, we'd have to dry-lot her—place her in a small dirt-only compound and give her special feed. We did that for a week, and Snow seemed irritated and depressed, along with barely being able to walk. She had no herd, which probably made her nervous. Dusty phoned occasionally to say all Mike could talk about was who was taking care of Snow when he wasn't there, and how would he know someone was looking after her.

One day I went out to the dry lot to check on Snow, and Mike was standing there, talking to her and brushing her, and John, his veteran-buddy, was with him. No sign of Dusty. Snow seemed more relaxed and happy. I casually asked Mike how he got to the ranch, and he said they hitchhiked. I didn't say anything else but knew the VA posse would be hot on their trail.

Within minutes, Dusty's old Pontiac careened into the driveway, and she tumbled out like a load of laundry from the dryer. She was hot, out of breath, and upset. Mike and John were AWOL as far as the veterans' home was concerned, which jeopardized their ability to live there. That meant their families were upset, and now the veterans' home would have to place restrictions on their time outside the facility.

"It seems wrong," I said to Dusty. "They came out here because they were worried about the horse. Now, Mike in particular will be really worried because he can't even see her once a week." Dusty sympathized, but rules were rules. She loaded the two men into her car, and I told them not to worry, that I'd be sure to check on Snow every day, but I could see tears in the corner of Mike's eye.

❖

Later that afternoon, Margaret Windom came by to say she was surprised that Jane wasn't back, although she did love working with Wiley. "But then you must be proud of what Jane's accomplished." Margaret pulled out one of her infamous newspaper clippings. Jane was standing next to a pretty brunette about my age, with her arm slung over her shoulder and the headline *Barrow Still Has It*. It was a story about her performance in a small New Mexico town and how the people loved her for showing up. I wondered why she went out of her way for such a small community, but the girl in the photo had to be the reason. My mind completely left my body. She was back in the news hanging on women, leading her life as she always had. My mental absence gave Margaret space to move in. She took the clipping out of my hand, leaned in, and kissed me. I must have jumped a foot. "I can do better than that lying down," she said.

"Margaret, no, please. I'm not interested in a relationship with you."

"I can protect your reputation…" she cooed. "I'm discreet. She's not."

She strolled out, apparently having done what she came to do. Cal entered as Margaret was leaving.

"Margaret Windom just kissed me," I said, still stunned.

"Did you gargle with Lysol?" Cal laughed for the first time in weeks.

"She showed me a recent newspaper article about Jane's success in some New Mexico town, and there was a picture of her with her arm slung around this attractive, young, dark-haired woman." I expected Cal to defend Jane, but she didn't.

"Rae, I swear, we've gotten ourselves into a mutual mess. You suppose the two of them knew all along what they were doing when they moved in over there—just playing us for sex?"

"Did you have sex with Wiley?" I jumped at the chance to ask her.

"Why do you think I'm so mad…and hurt?" She looked more desolate than I could ever remember seeing her.

"Was it good?" I grinned.

"Spectacular. And just so you know, Jane told Wiley she had sex with you."

My face got hot. Jane Barrow telling people she'd had sex with me was the last straw. "I will never trust that woman again. In fact, I'll never see her."

"Before you blow out through the top of your head, it was in the context of why she'd lost ten pounds and couldn't remember where she'd left her truck keys."

"It doesn't matter what it was 'in the context of.' I'm never calling her again."

Cal plopped down in one of the office sling-chairs that could make you look slumped over, even on a good day, but today it practically put Cal in the fetal position. After a long pause, she said, "He's just so damned cute, and I love him."

"That's not good, unless he gets a divorce," I said. "But it's better than my situation. Jane's got a whole herd of admirers. She doesn't need a divorce as much as she needs to be shed-bladed to get all the loose women off her."

"Now we don't know that she's seeing a bunch of women." Cal made a halfhearted attempt to come to Jane's defense. "We *suspect* it. But although we're both suspicious women, we are fair, and we'll give anyone the benefit of the doubt until we know for sure—and then, once we know for sure, we'll cut their nuts off with a rusty razor."

"Jesus, Cal!" I said, crossing my legs quickly, despite having no anatomy in danger. "Don't be thinking like that!"

"Can't help it," she said. "He's hurt me to the core."

CHAPTER SEVENTEEN

It was hard to keep my promise to myself, but I was determined. *Imagine telling Wiley she'd had sex with me like she's some teenage boy racking up trophy points, then rolling off to New Mexico and cuddling up to a bunch of women.*

A couple of times my cell phone rang. It was Jane, but I didn't answer and, instead, just let the tears flow. A smart person doesn't get on a wild horse just to prove to herself she can ride it, unless she's willing to wear the scars.

I kept myself busy with the veterans' program. We had ten men signed up for horse interaction, and a waiting list, according to Dusty. But we only had two horses, and Snow was still recovering from her foundering, so she wasn't fully available even for walking and petting. Even with just a few veterans, the program consumed an entire day by the time you got everything set up, and if that took place every week, it would cut into our income, not to mention be too hard on the weakened horses. If we got three more horses with the necessary temperament, that would add to the cost of feed, vetting, and managing. So we had to draw the line on expansion until we knew if the grant would come through. It was thrilling that the program was working, and I loved greeting all the old veterans who were so happy to see the horses, but it broke my heart that we couldn't take more.

And I missed Mike. After all, he was the one who noticed Snow's foundering before anyone else, so I approached Dusty. "What if we could make a tiny weekly donation in exchange for his coming out and helping with the horses? It would be like a ranch internship. He could choose the days and the hours. Ellie would give him things to do, and that might change his status from veterans' home escapee to ranch helper." Dusty grinned at me and finally said they'd look into it with his family and figure out the transportation issue.

Cal and I sat at the table in the barn office and penciled out all the elements involved in the veterans' horse program. Assuming we had funds to do it, we could take a total of two dozen vets: twelve men on Tuesday working with four horses over three hours, and another twelve men on Thursday, which would give each man an hour with his individual horse. So we'd need two more rescue horses, money for vetting, feed costs, labor, and Cal's time, because we couldn't leave the men unsupervised with the horses, and then there was the overhead to compensate the ranch, because this program would be unending and perhaps even grow.

"It's just got a lot of moving parts." Cal sighed. "You need to find the additional horses and get them vetted and up to speed, but you don't want that expense if the program's not going to be funded."

"You should talk to your friends who brought us Snow and Beauty, tell them what we're thinking."

"Once you bite down on this, you know there's no turning back. Cuz if you quit or the funding dries up, you'll have old petting horses out the ass!"

I stared at her for a moment, then burst out laughing, "You have such a way with words."

It was late afternoon when I got the call from Dusty saying the grant wouldn't happen. We didn't meet the criteria for submission. I have to admit I was deflated. The project had excited me. I'd already envisioned women veterans and maybe special training that would ultimately allow some of the more able vets to be led around the ring on a horse. So, I had to get it out of my head, but when I did, Jane popped into the space it vacated. I missed her terribly but couldn't think about that.

Even if we could fund the horse program through private sources, we would still need to meet a lot of governmental criteria and have licensed physical therapists on hand—at least that's what I imagined—all of which cost money. I was walking through the barn thinking about how to make the project work without a grant when Margaret appeared.

"Cal told me about your little project," she crooned, and I noticed she was dressed differently, a little more provocatively, her blouse low cut and one extra button open as if by accident revealing a lace bra. Her pants were tight, and she wore expensive cowboy boots, which almost made me laugh because, first of all, she couldn't ride, and second, if she could, she would definitely be wearing knee-high English riding boots. So I was pretty sure the new wardrobe was for me. I stood in the center of the aisle to make sure I had room to get away from her and wasn't trapped in any small spaces.

"I have the money to make that happen. And I would be delighted to be your deep-pocket donor, provided we became…deep partners," she said, emphasizing "deep," and my mind went to cavernous places in Margaret Windom where I didn't want to go.

"What are you proposing?" I asked, deciding to make her say it out loud.

"That you're the woman I visit when my husband is traveling. I make him happy, and he wants me to be happy." She casually moved toward me.

"Visit, as in your being here at the ranch to help run the program—"

She grabbed me, and I pulled back, but Margaret must have had a gym membership, because she was strong, and she held me there as she kissed me, plunging her tongue into my mouth and then pulling away.

"Visit as in coming over to fuck you," she said in a gravelly whisper. "You like to fuck, don't you?" Her eyes were glazed over and, frankly, frightening, like she was off her medication. "And in our case, fucking one another solves a lot of problems for both of us."

It was as if she'd just discovered the word fuck and got off repeating it. I jerked away from her as Cal entered the barn.

"I'm sorry," Cal said, her voice loaded with surprise. "Am I interrupting?"

"Just a business discussion, Cal, about my funding the veterans' horse program and being more personally involved to help Rae."

Shocked, I just stood there like an idiot. I'd had people hit on me before, but no one in broad daylight shouting "fuck me." But then Margaret had money, and that seemed to let her think she could do, or say, anything.

"Well, I'll be in touch, Rae. And I enjoyed it."

She swung her hips out of the barn and across to her car.

"Holy shit. Did I hear her say fucking would solve a lot of problems for both of you? Did she actually say 'fucking'? She goes crazy when someone says damn. And was she kissing you? This is bad, Rae. We need the money if you want to save the program, but I can't see wanting any program enough to fuck Margaret Windom."

I pulled myself back to reality and began to giggle. "Have you ever…?"

Cal doubled over laughing, suggesting I could pay off the

entire ranch, start the veterans' program, and a million other things if I could just become less picky about who I slept with.

"Speaking of which," she said slyly, "have you talked to Jane?"

"Not for weeks."

"Well, I talked to Wiley. She's put the ranch up for sale."

I almost collapsed from the shock of never seeing Jane again. "Why in the hell would she do that?" I asked.

"Maybe because she thinks it's over with you, and it would be too painful to come back here if that's true."

"Or maybe this is her way of getting me to call her and beg her not to do it, so she can keep me on the string, manipulate me, which is what she does. She's got a girl at every arena, like she's the cutting-horse-cuties champion. Well, I'm not falling for it. If she wants to sell her ranch, fine. Then we just sit here and wait for idiot number six to buy the damned thing."

"Thanks for what you did with Wiley." She changed the subject. "He filed for divorce." She paused for a long time while she worked up to what came next. "When it's final, he wants me to marry him."

"Oh, but meantime, he wants you to fuck him on the promise he'll marry you, right? Why buy the cow when the milk's so cheap? They're two of a kind, Cal. Don't get sucked into it."

I was aware that I'd ruined her announcement. She was happy, and hopeful, and I'd crushed her good news like it was a cockroach. I didn't know what to say to apologize, but Cal spoke first.

"You know, Rae, at some point you've got to trust someone. And if you can't do that, at least trust your gut instinct. Because if you're going to stay like this, well, you're going to be alone forever."

Cal's eyes were tearing up, and she walked away, making

me feel horrible. Now I was in deep shit. No Jane Barrow to love in the night. Some crazy new neighbor to argue with. No head of my riding school, because Cal would probably run off with Wiley. I felt like one of those buildings where they carefully plant explosives inside, a crowd gathers to watch, they count down the seconds, and then the whole thing implodes, nothing left but dust.

I sat down to think about what Cal had said. Why didn't I trust anybody? Maybe it was because my dad left when I was four. Or because my mother, who couldn't handle his leaving, left me, giving me to my grandmother, who told people she was too old to raise a kid. Or maybe it happened the day my grandmother told me my mother was in the hospital and wouldn't be coming to see me ever again, because her liver was gone. I was an only child, so I didn't have anyone to ask about where her liver went. It had just left like everything else. I had no one to cry with. I could tap into the hurt of that day like a rhythm section on the radio, but I'd learned to turn the dial, and I didn't want to listen to it ever again.

CHAPTER EIGHTEEN

I looked at Jane's phone number several times, but I kept myself from calling by envisioning the little chick in the newspaper climbing into bed with her, or more likely necking in her SUV. I also kept watch on her ranch and noticed Wiley had moved the cattle out. I guess no need to keep steers if you're not actually using them for anything. Jane had Dark Horse so, as far as I could tell, Howie was the only horse Wiley was riding, and maybe two or three other horses he used for working with kids like Belle.

Occasionally I'd spot someone mowing a pasture, or fixing a fence, or tending to some building repair, but by and large it looked like they were fixing it up for sale. I went online and found it listed under *Barrow Ranch for Sale ten million dollars.* I laughed out loud. *If they sell that ranch for ten million dollars, she can stick her Stetson up my ass! This proves she's just baiting me, trying to get me to call her.*

My phone rang, my heart leapt, but it was Margaret Windom. She got right to the point. "I owe you a huge apology. I don't know what came over me. My medication lately has been off-kilter. Anyway, not to bore you with that, but it won't happen again, I can assure you. That kind of language is *not* me."

I thanked her, glad she'd straightened that out.

"My brother was a veteran," she said in a very businesslike tone. "I am interested in launching this program in his honor. Are you interested?"

The word "interested" was loaded with meaning, but she'd just told me that she was apologizing, so maybe I was reading more into the word than was there.

"You know I am looking for a way to fund the program," I said, "but I have to tell you, Margaret, that I won't sleep with you to get that done."

She laughed, and I had to admit, I thought her laugh was charming. "Okaaay." She dragged the word out seductively. "I thought we'd just cleared that up. Let's make an agreement. I will give you enough money to fund the program for a year, if you have dinner at my home and simply explain the program in detail, so I can share it with my husband. He'll want to understand what we'd be supporting." I paused for so long, she asked, "Are you still there?"

"Yes," I said, as to my being on the line, but she quickly took my response to mean we had a dinner date.

"I will have a car pick you up. That way, if we have a glass of wine, you won't be on the highway afterward. And I will give you the driver's name and number, so you're in control of when you leave. Loosen up. It will be fun."

"Okay, when?"

"Tonight?"

Margaret was nothing if not organized, and I couldn't think of a better, or worse, night, so I agreed, then hung up, nervously contemplating what I'd just committed to do. I was deep in thought, rationalizing the dinner, when Cal came by to talk about the purchases we needed to make for the horses: wormer, bute, and grain.

"I can't talk long. I have to go get ready for dinner with

Margaret Windom." I smiled at her. The look on Cal's face was worth the evening I was facing. "She's promised me a year of funding if I'll come to her home, have dinner, and simply explain the program so she can share the details with her husband."

"Now, Rae, you aren't that naive. Margaret Windom isn't going to let you out of her house until she gets what she wants, so I hope you're ready to fork it over."

"I have it all under control," I said, and went back to the house to find the appropriate outfit to wear—something nice but not seductive. I selected dark-blue slacks, a blue western shirt, beige boots and belt, and a gold choker made of 14K running horses. I looked somewhere between country casual and dinner out. Pacing nervously, I wondered how to even start a business, much less social, conversation with Margaret.

The town car arrived at six p.m. sharp. The driver stepped out and held the door for me. I confirmed his number and name, and said I'd be calling him later to pick me up. He nodded, saying he had the address of the Windom residence. I sat back, pushing deep into the padded seats, trying to regulate my breathing, not having done anything like this, well, ever.

The neighborhood, a forty-minute drive from the ranch, was nothing but big estate homes that looked like oil barons owned them. Each two-story house occupied at least a sprawling, manicured acre or two and was constructed of stone and brick, bespeaking the perceived permanence of wealth. The driver pulled into the circular drive of a huge mansion, got out, and opened the town-car door for me, telling me to enjoy my evening.

I stood on the steps next to two gargantuan urns with exotic plants sprouting from them and rang the doorbell, feeling self-conscious. A middle-aged, heavy-set woman in an apron, wearing a cross of turquoise stones, opened the door and welcomed me inside, introducing herself as Mrs. Windom's personal assistant. She had kind eyes and looked motherly, perhaps Hispanic, I thought, as she led me to a parlor just to the right of the entrance, and we exchanged pleasantries.

"Have you worked for Mrs. Windom long?" I asked her, and she said she'd worked there for ten years. "That's a long time. She must be a really nice woman." I was seeking reassurance. Her assistant hesitated for a second before nodding, and for a moment, I thought I detected sadness in her eyes, but maybe that came from having to live modestly and work in someone's mansion. Who knew what was waiting for her at home—an ill son she supported perhaps, or an elderly mother. Who would ever know? She was just the assistant, the servant, but at least the surroundings in which she worked were beautiful.

No sooner had she left than Margaret swept into the room. She was wearing a silky mauve pantsuit with flowing legs and arms, and I felt like I was in the wrong outfit.

"Don't you look darling, darling." She laughed.

"You look lovely as well," I said, and she gave me a cheek kiss by way of greeting.

"Sit," she commanded, putting me on a plush black-velvet couch, then sitting down a few feet away. "Tell me about your program."

Our evening had the feeling of a business meeting, but everything surrounding it felt like anything but business. I was having trouble syncing the tense mother of Sara Belle with this much looser, lovelier lady. I explained the entire program to her, and she interrupted only to ask questions about things like staffing, liability, and goals. When we got to the finances, she suggested I put my request in writing, when I got back to the ranch, and send it to her. She would have her accountant cut me a check. I thanked her and asked where Sara Belle was. She explained that she was on an overnight with her girlfriends. Then she told a funny story about chaperoning her daughter and four other teenage girls at the school dance, when no one could dance, and she imitated their awkward moves. "The balloons and music were the only clues that they weren't experiencing a mass seizure," she said, and I laughed in spite of myself.

When I mentioned her husband, she relished the topic and seemed very proud of everything he'd accomplished. He was an engineer, and he traveled constantly, mostly to third-world countries, working out infrastructure issues for better and cleaner water that would reach tiny villages. After hearing her description of his work, and her admiration for him, I relaxed, thinking this wouldn't be the kind of evening I'd dreaded, but perhaps something nicer.

She poured me a glass of wine from a crystal carafe, and we drank, and she told funny stories about her travels abroad. She had a great sense of humor.

In an hour, her assistant came in and said dinner was served. We walked past a huge dining room, with a dozen gold chairs with equestrian hunt scenes on them, to a sitting room with a small table set for two, overlooking a pool that seemed to be part of the room as if we were in a cove on some Greek isle. The effect was amazing and I told her so, but she brushed off my compliment as if the expense and creativity involved in creating this little nook meant nothing to her. The dinner consisted of small filets and vegetables, along with homemade bread. Margaret poured more wine and was pleasantly tipsy. I found myself really enjoying the evening. Having a patron dinner occasionally might be fun.

After dinner was cleared away, her assistant asked if we needed anything more, and Margaret thanked her and dismissed her.

"Take your boots off, and let's dangle our feet in the water, watch the moon, and solve all the world's problems." She kicked off her flats, and we walked to the edge of the pool and sat on cabana mats, putting our feet in the water. I was vaguely aware that if we leaned back, we would be on a mattress, but my head was spinning. In fact, she suggested we lie back so we could see the stars, and she gave me a little push, and I flopped back as she caught my drink.

Then, as I lay there, Margaret Windom took her clothes off, all of them at lightning speed. She was totally naked beside me and took my hand and placed it on her breast, but my arm fell away. I tried to get up, but it felt like someone had put a fifty-pound weight on my chest. Then, as if in a fog, I had the sensation that I was being pulled back from the pool, and then my pants were being tugged off, but I wasn't able to move my arms or legs to resist. The feeling was incredibly frightening, because I couldn't think, and I was physically paralyzed. Then Margaret was on top of me, doing exactly what she'd whispered to me in the barn that she wanted to do. She kept looking up at someone, a man sitting there, tall and bald, wearing glasses, and he was watching us from a lounge chair, jerking himself off. Could that be true? Did I make that up? I passed out.

When I woke up, I was naked and covered in a blanket. Margaret was smiling at me, offering me coffee, and the sun had come up. She was stroking me. "Did you have a good time, sweetheart?"

"What happened?"

"You had a little too much to drink. That's what happened."

"You drugged me. I couldn't move my arms or legs, and I couldn't think. And someone else was here."

"No remorse." She kissed me, and I tried to push her away and get my clothes on. "I phoned Cal and told her you'd had a lot to drink, and you were staying over, and not to worry about you. The check will be in the mail for the program." Then she patted my butt as she left the room. Her assistant came in to tell me the car was waiting, but she kept her head down, refusing to look at me, as if she knew something about my sleepover was out of the ordinary. And that's how I ended my stay at the Windom mansion.

On the drive home, I caught the driver looking at me in the rearview mirror. The plague of a small town—he was the same guy who'd dropped me off. *Does he know what happened? After all, I never phoned him to pick me up last night, and I didn't put on new makeup or even brush my hair, so I must look like a woman who's been "rode hard and put up wet."*

When the town car pulled into the ranch, I got out, not waiting for the driver to hold the door for me. Cal came running as he drove away.

"What in the hell happened?" she yelped.

Silent tears flowed down my cheeks. "You were right. She drugged me and raped me. And a man was there. I don't know what he did."

"No! Oh, my God! We have to report it." She didn't move toward me to hug me or comfort me. She must have sensed that I didn't want anyone to touch me.

I gave her a cynical laugh. "I assume that's why it works for her. To report it would be to say I'm a lesbian. And no one in Oklahoma would believe that a fine, upstanding, wealthy woman like Mrs. Windom drugs and rapes lesbians. The report would read that a lesbian businesswoman tried to blackmail community benefactor, Mrs. Margaret Windom. The lesbian, Rae Starr, runs a riding school for young girls. One client, when interviewed, remarked that she'd always thought Ms. Starr's anti-family, anti-religious stance wasn't the best fit for impressionable young women. Then they'll run me out of business. Meanwhile, Mrs. Windom will be on record as donating all the money for the launch of the Veterans' Horse Program and adoring her brilliant, philanthropist husband. Now how could she be a rapist? And how ungrateful and depraved is this Rae Starr woman?"

"What are you going to do?" Cal asked, somberly.

"Cash her fucking check. Call the program the Margaret Windom Veterans' Horse Program, so she has to fund it every year."

"I don't think that's a good plan, Rae. It just lets the two of them do the same thing to other women."

"I doubt there are other women. It would be hard to find even one other woman as stupid and gullible as I am." My anger welled up, and I stormed off, heading for the house and leaving Cal outside.

I went into the bathroom and took an extra-long shower. If the man had raped me, then I was washing away the evidence, but I didn't care. No one would believe my story anyway, and it was more important that I wash them off me. I felt dirty. And in between my legs I was sore, almost beaten up. God knows what she'd used on me or had done to me. I started crying again. The shower was the perfect place for tears.

CHAPTER NINETEEN

The check arrived almost immediately without my having to send an itemized statement for her accountant. Margaret Windom was buying silence. Cal began to work on getting the rescue horses, and Dusty was organizing the program from her end. I was still depressed over how we'd gotten the money, and I was embarrassed. Margaret Windom called, but I didn't answer the phone. I never wanted to see or speak to her again.

This time it was Cal who brought me the present-day internet story about Jane. "She's busting her butt to be everywhere and resurrect her heyday. Looks like it's working, I guess." Cal was trying to get me interested in Jane again, but the articles were having the opposite effect.

When Jane began to pop up on Twitter and Instagram, I was sure some little honey in her entourage was helping her with all those postings, but I didn't say anything.

It was a bright summer morning, and temperatures had dropped to a mild eighty degrees. Fall would soon be here, and I was eager to forget the heat of summer. The attack by Margaret Windom had changed me, maybe even hardened me in some way. I was coming to grips with the fact that I lived in a world where perverts could disguise themselves as benefactors and upstanding citizens, and be loved and accepted, while, if I wanted any respect at all, I had to disguise myself as a straight woman who simply hadn't found the right guy. Everyone should have to own who they are, for their own health and well-being, I thought.

"So what would you think if I let all our students' parents know that I'm a lesbian, and we begin weeding out those clients who have a problem with that fact?" I asked Cal.

"What do you mean? Post a sign in the barn that says, 'Lesbian owned and operated'?"

"What happened to me has made me think not living my truth leaves me open to blackmail. Of course, living my truth in Oklahoma could leave me open to bankruptcy, but I'm worn out with the game. Who do you think would have a problem with knowing I'm a lesbian?"

"Everyone. All the kids with evangelical parents, for sure. You know how it goes. A friend tells a student's mother that being around you will make her kid gay, and the mother gets so freaked, she spills grape juice on her autographed picture of Jesus Christ and quits the barn."

"But with the veterans' program, would we offset the losses?" I asked.

"We might. I'll have to figure it out. I have an idea. Now don't yell until I finish. When you have to deliver news some people feel is bad, you start with good news, slip in the bad news, and follow it with good news. Kind of a 'good-news sandwich.' Sooo, the good news is that we're holding an open house. During the event we let our clientele know, casually, that you're a champion of diversity. Then we follow that news with Jane Barrow is coming to the ranch to do a three-day cutting-horse clinic and our students are invited for free."

"You're as manipulative as she is. How would you contact her?" My heart rate was automatically increasing with just the idea of seeing her again.

"Wiley knows where she is."

I paused a long time. "Do what you want," I said, and walked off. Cal charged out of the office, jumped into the truck, and hightailed it over to the Barrow Ranch. She was gone past dark. When she didn't return, I poured myself a glass of wine on the porch. Jane and I hadn't been in communication since I'd seen the press clipping of her with her arm around yet another woman. Maybe the event would just reset the table, get us back to being friends. It would be unbearable just being Jane Barrow's friend. I'd rather never see her again.

The following morning Cal brought me her plan. An event to announce two big programs: the Veterans' Horse Program and the upcoming Jane Barrow Cutting-Horse Clinic.

People would be invited for cocktails, and Cal would make the formal announcement about the Veterans' Horse Program and talk about diversity and inclusion, and how progressive our stable is in preparing young women to meet the world. "After I finish you'll be free to be who you are…whoever that is," she joked.

"So you're handling everything," I said, happy that she was.

"Well, you can't just mentally check out. I'll tee it up, and then you have to make a little speech, which I'll write for you, so you don't say anything that spooks the herd."

"What about Jane?"

"I've spoken to the person handling the tour, and she says Jane will do it, but she has to be paid."

"Are you kidding me? You think I'm paying Jane-fucking-Barrow to appear here?"

"It's three days, Rae, and she has to pay her staff, okay? She said she'll do her part for free. Man, you're difficult to deal with."

❖

Cal and Wiley were scurrying around like it was the Mad Hatter's tea party, the event seeming to have provided a legitimate reason for them to spend every minute together. They were figuring out if people stood and drank, or sat and drank, or got a meal, or just finger food, and who got to speak and who didn't, and who was invited and who wasn't. I was sure that Wiley could have given a rat's ass about any of this, other than it gave him intimate hours with Cal. The two of them looked cute together—roughly the same height, bouncy and buoyant—and Cal lit up when she was around him.

They'd ironed out most of the details by the time Cal came up to the porch to have a talk and fill me in. She described where things would go and how the evening would flow, and then she got to the point. "You know, we have to invite Margaret Windom."

I bounced out of my chair. "I don't want her anywhere near here!"

"She *is* the benefactor, and the program's named after her, so there's no way she's not going to show up. Look, I knew what your reaction would be, and God knows I don't blame you, but it's either talk it through now or surprise you with her arrival."

"You'd better never do that to me—never surprise me with Margaret Windom!"

"She's not going to jump out of a cake, for God's sake. There will be no surprises, which is why I'm sitting here and we're having this talk, if you can call it that."

"Is she going to speak?" I nearly shouted, and Cal didn't say anything, which I knew was her way of saying what do you think, it's her money. "This is the worst mess I've ever been in."

I appreciated Cal holding her peace on that one, because

she could toss out a long list of messes we'd been in together. "Just keep her away from me." I was seething.

"I'll try," she replied. "Maybe tie her to the hitching post out back, although she'd probably like that." Cal laughed, and I smirked. I still hadn't gotten to a place in my heart where I could find any emotion, other than anger, on this topic.

"Jane asked how we talked Margaret Windom into putting up the money for the program's first year," Cal said.

"What did you tell her?"

"I told her Margaret Windom had a brother who was a vet, and she wanted to honor him."

I didn't say any more. Who knew if that was even true?

Cal left, and I sat mulling over the idea that I would see Margaret Windom at this event. What would I do? How would I behave? What would I say? I couldn't ignore her. She was the benefactor, so I couldn't dodge her.

For some reason my dilemma made me think of a young college friend back East. A male classmate raped her, but she never reported him and had to sit in class with him. I didn't fully appreciate what she'd been through. The penalty for rape should be castration, plain and simple. But of course, first you have to get someone to believe you, and that's where the rapist has the upper hand, because the only witness is you.

❖

Two weeks to the day, we were all set up for the event. Jane and her crew were to drive in at midday. We would have the cocktail party and announcement at our ranch that evening. Then the next morning, the cutting-horse clinic would begin at the Barrow Ranch. First day would include basic lessons, riding a horse with an electric flag programmed to zip around the arena and simulate a cow. The second day, participants would get a chance to work real cows that Wiley had to load back in. And the third day, Wiley would work with them and give Jane a break. We invited all students and parents, our sponsors and suppliers, which meant about a hundred invitations went out. Cal was smart to sprinkle in sponsors and suppliers, because they tended to be more liberal, business taking precedence over political or religious beliefs.

Jane's entourage pulled in around noon at her ranch, and I raced into the house and began trying on outfits, like I thought I was going to be in a cover shoot for *Cowgirl Magazine*. About an hour later, Jane's big, black Expedition pulled into the drive, and my heart stopped. She got out wearing exactly what she'd worn the first time I laid eyes on her. She moved more slowly, as if afraid she might spook me, but the charm was cascading off her. The hat, the belt buckle, the long slender hands with the trophy ring, the way she moved—I was frozen.

"Rae, I've really missed you," she said. I walked slowly toward her and meant to give her a quick welcome-home hug, but it turned into a vise grip. She wrapped her arms around me, my head on her chest, and just stood there rocking me like a baby. Tears gathered in my eyes. "I don't know where to begin," she said.

"Don't say anything. Just hold me." She was still holding me when Cal came up.

"You two want to take that inside before I have to explain to Mrs. Remington that you're actually cousins," she said, her eyes darting in all directions, apparently in search of horrified heterosexuals, as I walked Jane into the living room and right into the bedroom, and locked the door.

I couldn't get her clothes off fast enough, and I was on her like white on rice, kissing every part of her and running my hands over her as if she were a horse I was thinking of buying.

Her legs and arms were so tight and her butt firm. It was still daylight, so I could see every mark on her, every scrape, every beautiful piece of her, nothing to hide, and she was seeing me fully for the first time as well.

"The scar on your hip from the bull is so deep," I said, caressing her.

"Like a lot of wounds," she replied, and I loved her for surviving the pain of her youth. She turned back over and slid her hand between my legs, and I jumped and pulled back.

"You okay?" She stopped everything.

"Yes." I tried to kiss her to avoid more questions.

But she sensed something was wrong. "What's going on? Tell me. Something's changed." I started to cry. "You are so beautiful, Rae. Talk to me."

"I can't right now." I sobbed. "And we have people coming for this event."

"Let's slow down. Get through this evening. No rush." And for a while she just held me, and rocked me back and forth, and kissed my hair, and I felt loved...and ashamed.

A soft knock at the bedroom door, and Cal's voice said, "Ladies, we are one hour from the cocktail party, so I humbly recommend you get your cock tails out of the sack and get dressed."

We both suppressed giggles.

"Thanks, Cal. Is the coast clear for Jane to get back to her SUV without questions about why she has no boots or pants?" I teased her.

"Coast is clear if you go now. But hustle up. I'd like to make the announcement that you're a lesbian, rather than have everyone discover it by finding you both naked."

Jane leapt up, grabbed her boots, and belt, and hat, and pulled her pants and shirt on. "I'm coming back for more." She kissed me so long I almost decided to hell with the party, but I couldn't do that to Cal. After she left, and I heard her cross the living room, I jumped into the shower again.

At seven p.m., the cars started rolling in, full of older students and their parents and the people who were here for the cutting-horse clinic. I put on my best outfit for no one else but Jane—all buckskin and blue. Jane showed up looking startlingly gorgeous. The glow between us was hard to conceal, and we stood as close to one another as we could. Suddenly, I looked up, and Margaret Windom was headed my way wearing what appeared to be a very expensive and subdued black suit that gave her an aura of "conservative society matron."

"Keep her away from me," I hissed at Cal, and I was sure Jane heard me.

Cal spoke as if reminding a child, "The vet program, as you recall, is the Margaret Windom Veteran's Horse Program. She's here because she wrote the check, remember?"

"I paid for the damned program," I muttered.

Margaret came floating over, as if on air, and flung herself at me, saying she'd missed me. I disentangled myself from her immediately. My reaction wasn't lost on Jane, who backed away a few steps. "So you're back, you wanderlust," Margaret teased Jane.

"Doing the clinic for Rae," Jane said, and I could hear her mind churning.

I glanced over Margaret's shoulder at the man driving her car, who was stepping out to join her. He was tall, bald, and wore glasses, and I was momentarily paralyzed again. He was the man who'd faded in and out of my consciousness that fateful night. Margaret waved him over, and my knees grew weak.

"Rae, this is my wonderful husband, Steve Windom, whom I've told you so much about, and our co-sponsor of the program."

He looked pleasant, and distinguished, and he extended his hand. "So nice to meet you. I've heard so many good things about you." I couldn't make any words. I felt so freaked out I thought I'd faint.

Cal took over, welcoming them and asking Ellie to get them drinks. Wiley was on hand, and Cal waved him over to join the conversation. He chatted up the Windoms with enthusiasm, allowing me to escape.

Jane leaned over and asked me if I was okay, obviously sensing that I wasn't. All I could say was "fine," but I wasn't, and she knew I wasn't.

"Do you know that guy?" Cal whispered, gesturing toward Steve Windom.

"He was the guy at the pool with her that night," I replied.

"Her husband is Mr. Jerk Off? Holy shit." But we didn't have time to discuss that. About 7:45 p.m., Cal gathered everyone up, turned on a small hand mic, and said we were so happy they'd come for this special evening.

Somewhere in her speech, she said, "As you know, Rae Starr, who owns and operates this ranch and stable, is a person who believes in, and practices, diversity and inclusion. Our students are African American, Native American, and we now have military veterans, single moms, and, as most of you know, Rae herself is a lesbian."

I saw one mother's head snap back as she leaned into the woman next to her asking for clarification. "Did she say thespian or lesbian?"

"So it only makes sense," Cal said more forcefully, "that we continue in that vein creating a program for veterans, men and women who fought for our country and are now fighting depression. This program lets us fight for them."

Cal then thanked Dusty Daniels and explained that she'd conducted a small trial at the ranch a few months ago, and it proved that veterans interacting with horses on a regular basis become happier and mentally healthier. Then she launched into what expanding that program entailed and how we could never have accomplished it alone. "That's when our benefactor, philanthropist Margaret Windom, stepped up, and in honor of her brother, who was a veteran, funded the program for a minimum of one year." Everyone burst into applause and whistled, and Margaret was delighted. She stepped up and took the microphone.

"Thank you. My husband, Steve, and I love to contribute to worthwhile endeavors, and what could be more worthwhile than veterans getting mentally stronger by working with horses. And, of course, I want to thank the lovely, and kind, Miss Rae Starr for shepherding this ranch, and this program. She came to see me and asked for my help, and I must say she was incredibly persuasive." She gave me a coy glance, as if the two of us had a little secret, which in fact we did, and I wanted to throw something at her. "I simply couldn't say no to her." She gave me a scorching look and a little bow, and I gave her a weak smile and wave. I took the mic and, completely out of my body, thanked her, and then I thanked Dusty for conceiving the program and Cal for helping us run it. Finally, Cal took over and said we had something very special to announce.

"Cutting-horse champion Jane Barrow has left her tour to come back here to the Barrow Ranch and conduct a clinic on cutting-horse basics, which we are offering free to our students. So for those of you who signed up, beginning tomorrow morning at seven a.m., you'll be in the chow line at the Barrow ranch, and then in the arena at eight a.m. Please enjoy the rest of the evening with us, and feel free to go out and see the horses. And, thank you for being part of the Rae Starr Ranch."

Margaret was in my face the minute the mic was dead.

"Such an exciting night. I'm thrilled over the program." She stroked my arm, petting me as if I were her poodle, and I pulled away.

"We are too," I said flatly.

"I can see this rolling out into a national effort. It could grow into something powerful and important. How about dinner tomorrow night to discuss?"

Is she serious? The woman drugged and raped me, and now it's just "pass the biscuits, please"?

"I don't know if you caught the announcement, but I was just introduced as a lesbian, which means I will undoubtedly lose a few clients. And you probably don't want an out lesbian coming to see you for dinner, when your husband's out of town, which apparently he never is, but just in a lounge chair having himself, while I'm paralyzed, and being assaulted, and thinking I'm about to die," I said with disdain. "I don't want to attend another dinner where you drug and rape me, Margaret. Why don't you just have sex with a mannequin," I hissed quietly.

"I don't know what you're talking about!" She drew back, feigning utter shock. "And if you harbor some inexplicable animosity toward me or my husband, maybe I shouldn't be funding this program."

"Don't even think of backing out." I smiled through my teeth. "I paid for this program." I turned and walked off.

I could hear Jane across the lawn talking to several men about cutting horses. One of them was Steve Windom, who was up to his ears in beers, regaling her with his bronc-riding abilities in college and how he'd won the school trophy at Cal Poly. I was disgusted that he would put his bronc-riding skills up against all Jane had done. The evening dragged on, although everyone seemed to love it—looking at the stars, petting the horses, and drinking under the moonlight. It was apparent Jane and I weren't going to see each other tonight. She saluted me as she drifted off to her car, and I ached for her touch.

Everyone left all at once. Cal came up to ask me how I thought it went, and I told her she did a great job.

"You must have fucked Barrow's brains out. Her eyes were lit up like LCDs," Cal said, and I didn't dissuade her from that romantic notion. I didn't want to say that what had really happened was intense cuddling, because that didn't sound nearly as sexy.

Instead, I said, "I had to deal with Margaret Windom, and I think Jane knew something was up. She didn't bother to stay afterward."

"Or maybe she drove all day, made love all afternoon, has an early morning, and she's fifty, you think?" she said, and I smiled.

A text came over my phone. "Sorry to run. Come see the clinic in the morning, and save tomorrow night for me." I grinned so wide that Cal couldn't resist.

"I assume that's more text-sex with JB. If things get any hotter, you two could go up in flames."

Chapter Twenty

I drove over to the Barrow Ranch in time to see adoring kids standing in a circle around Jane taking instructions on cutting-horse basics. She was charismatic, and the young women in the crowd stared at her like she was a rock star. One starry-eyed teen asked Jane if she gave private lessons, and Jane cut Wiley an amused look. "Never a lesson without Wiley, but I do work with students in very small groups." I started to move away, and Jane quickly turned the questions over to Wiley, saying out loud, "Rae, wait a minute, please."

She was standing next to me almost immediately and had me by the arm, gently propelling me up the steps and into the house, stopping in the ranch kitchen just off the porch and out of sight of anyone outdoors.

"You didn't tell me what that Windom woman did to you." She was visibly upset. I ducked my head. "That's what was going on with you last night." I started to say something, but tears welled up. "Did you see a doctor? Do you have an attorney?"

"I'm not filing charges. No one would believe me, and it would wreck my business. How did you find out?"

"Doesn't matter. I found out."

"Now every time I think of making love, I think of that, and it ruins it. I feel like everything in me is ruined."

"I could kill those two," Jane said, and her voice held a quiet anger I'd never heard before.

"I'll get over it. I just have to get my head on straight."

Jane didn't say anything. She just held me, and I whimpered like a baby and then felt stupid for making her nice shirt wet and for not being able to suck it up. "It was my fault. I went to her house knowing—"

"Not your fault. Because you go to someone's house for dinner, and to talk about funding a program, doesn't mean you're inviting a rape. Rae, rape changes you unless you take charge and turn the tables on the rapist. Otherwise that rape stays with you like a disease you can't quit thinking about, can't talk about, and can't cure. We have to decide what you're going to do."

"What did you do, when it happened to you?"

"I was fourteen. It was decades ago. There wasn't much to do. I had the baby. And my entire family thought I'd seduced a nice older man, gotten pregnant, and was a slut. The way that made me feel stuck with me for years, and if I think about it too long, I can still experience that feeling of it being my fault."

"Well, nothing's changed in thirty-five years about anyone believing the victim. At least not here in Oklahoma."

I could hear Wiley shouting Jane's name in the background as people applauded, and she said, "Gotta go, but we'll be together tonight. I promise."

Cal walked in to confirm that Wiley needed Jane in the arena.

"You told Jane," I said softly, still drying my tears.

"No. I told Wiley."

"Same thing," I said.

"Well, I'm not sorry I did. You need some help with this.

And while we're at it, I told her about your family growing up, because I know you sure didn't."

"None of that was yours to tell," I said.

"Yeah, well, Jane deserves to know that you think she'll leave you, because growing up everybody did. It's only fair she knows what she's working with here."

"And what's that, Dr. Phil?" I was angry.

"More than I'd want to deal with, that's for damn sure." Cal stormed out.

I walked out, got in my truck, and drove back to my ranch, tears of anger rolling down my cheeks. I was mad at Cal, mad that I got mad at Cal, and mad at myself mostly. *What kind of goddamned fool am I? Did I think it would just be beef Wellington and big bucks? Did I think I could play along to a point and get the funding? Did I encourage what happened by accepting the invitation?* I threw myself onto my bed and cried myself to sleep.

It was nine p.m. when Jane came over. She had the kindest expression I'd ever seen on her face. It reminded me of the way she'd looked at the two broken and starved white mares the first time she laid eyes on them. She walked into the bedroom and casually slipped out of her clothes, hanging them on a hanger like she lived here. She was so beautiful standing there in the lamplight. Then she helped me out of my clothes, and we slid into bed naked, and she held me.

"Rae Starr, I love you with all my heart." It was the last thing she said to me before her mouth was all over me. She didn't as much make love as she feasted on me, taking her time and her talented tongue, and massaging me into climax. I was shaking from head to toe and didn't know if I'd ever be able to stand up again. The power of her lovemaking was in her gentleness, her caring for how I felt. And I loved her for it. I buried my face between her legs and turned her into a quivering river of longing. When we came up for air, I knew she'd helped wipe away the negative feelings about what had happened to me. She was washing me clean.

"If you love me so much, why did you put the ranch up for sale?" I murmured.

"To get you to call me, but you're so damned stubborn you wouldn't," she said quietly.

"I knew that's what you were up to," I said dreamily. "I know you, Jane Barrow. I know you more than you know yourself."

"I was desperate to get your attention. I took it off the market," she said.

"Even so, you're going back to a different life. Announcer on the circuit, Wiley tells me. Interviews. A book deal. I don't want a long-distance romance. You and I missed our chance."

"Now wait a minute. You're skipping over an awful lot of things here."

"You're a celebrity, and you're traveling with a bunch of girls who swoon over you, and you're out at night in hotels, and casinos, and ballrooms. I would never trust you, couldn't depend on you, and would be alone without you. I'm not a gambler!"

"Now that's a lot of stuff to process. In your mind I've already left you, spent the night at some rock concert, gambled till dawn, slept with a bunch of women, lied to you, and never showed up. Do you really think that?"

"You should read your own press," I said, and she paused as if thinking about that.

"Why don't you come with me?"

"So I could keep an eye on you and constantly ask what in hell you think you're doing? I think it's better that I just be the woman in Oklahoma you see when you come back to the ranch." She ignored that comment and kissed me into another lovemaking session.

At dawn, Jane got dressed without a word, then leaned over and kissed me once more. "I don't want you to be the woman in Oklahoma. I want you to be the only woman I ever see. I'll finish the tour, but I'll be waiting for you. Every time someone walks through the door, I'll be hoping it's you." And she left.

How does she think that would work? I fretted and tossed after she left. I couldn't just leave my ranch, and my business, and trail after her from gig to gig. If she loved me, she'd make this her home and be here. *But it looks like her ranch is just going to be a place where she touches down occasionally.*

The clinic was in its third day, but Jane had already left to get back to her appearances. Just knowing she was gone put me in a funk.

Cal was ebullient over the entire three days, which had accomplished its goal of "outing" me to my clients. We had also garnered enough press online that we'd increased the number of people phoning to inquire about lessons—despite the revelation that we were, as Cal teased, "officially lesbian owned and operated." And of course the cutting-horse clinic with Jane had been a huge hit, and we were referring callers to Wiley.

"Margaret Windom rang, giddy over the entire evening and the possibility of a bigger veterans' program," Cal said. "She asked for you, but I said you weren't here, which is mentally true." Cal was in a friendly mood, having accepted my apology for my behavior.

"I hate that woman," I said quietly.

"I ran into Jane as she was leaving, and she asked me to take good care of you." Her voice was kind.

"I can take care of myself," I said, firmly.

"Yeah. We can all see how well that's going." She turned her back on me, like the difficult mare she was, and walked off.

Chapter Twenty-one

I focused on my business like I never had in my life—putting all the lust and love, and anger and energy, into getting this horse program for veterans up and running. Dusty reported back every week, telling me about changes in the men and women who were participating. One man barely spoke when his family came to visit him at the veterans' home, and now he carried on animated conversations about the horses, his in particular. Another started participating in stretching exercises, where before he was totally uninterested, even belligerent about exercising. He said he wanted to limber up so he could bend under the horse's belly and brush her, and care for her hooves. It was incredibly inspiring, the small ways in which horse therapy helped the veterans. I suggested we take photos of the horses and print them out, so they would have a picture of their horse to put up in their room.

Word of our success with the veterans spread, and I was pretty sure it was through Dusty. She and I made the local papers and were interviewed on the local TV stations. She said her phone rang off the hook with families wanting to get their loved ones into the program. Dusty documented all this and worked with a student at the university to write grant applications, and this time, we were almost certain to get them.

Cal and I still took riding clients, but only the ones Cal wanted. We weren't rich, but we were paying the bills and doing some good, and that helped heal my heartache and humiliation.

Nonetheless, particularly late at night when I was alone, I was in a dark, inexplicable depression.

Cal recognized it during the day, saying I didn't joke as much or have my usual spunk. It was kind of like the death of something. I could push it out of my mind, but then it would get triggered, like when Cal and I were talking on the porch about Belle, and how Wiley actually had her riding turn-back on Howie. Hearing about Belle brought up terrible thoughts of her mother, Margaret, and angry tears welled up.

Cal stopped mid-conversation. "Jane's right. You gotta do something to take your power back. This thing is eating you alive."

"Yeah, well, I'm cornered. How would you like to be Belle and hear that your mom is drugging and raping women? Your mom." I glared at Cal.

"And how can you be sure she doesn't already know that?"

I sat silent for a moment. Did Belle know? "Any step I take is horrible and hurtful, but the memories are eating me up. No one takes advantage of me. I'd shoot them! And then I walk right into this mess and let her do it. You were right. Somewhere in the back of my mind I must have known what happened was possible."

"Self-flagellation is not attractive and leaves scars, so stop it," Cal said, tired of my whining, I was certain.

I saw the gate opening, and one of the equestrian moms drove in, with her child in the front seat, and she headed for the parking area by the barn. Right behind her was another car I didn't recognize, until it got closer. It was Meg. She didn't have a working gate code, so she'd obviously waited outside the ranch gates until a car came through with a student, then followed it in. With students coming and going all day, it couldn't have been a long wait.

"Oh, for God's sake!" Cal threw her hands up in the air, signaling Meg's arrival was on a par with an invasion of locusts.

"I'm here to book a riding lesson." Meg grinned, getting out of her car.

"No available time," Cal said coldly, not finding Meg humorous.

"Would be nice if we could be friends this time around." She looked at Cal.

"There's not going to be another time around, so I'd appreciate it if you'd leave," I said.

"I'm moving back to town." That put the conversation on pause for about ten seconds. "My parents are having some health problems, and I can help out. They have that big house, and I can have the upstairs to myself. And I could see you occasionally."

"It's like having to call the exterminator again, because the rats are back." Cal stormed off. She'd never forgiven Meg for walking out on us and leaving me in debt. Not to mention Meg's infidelity, which was Cal's hot button, based on her own marital experience with her drunken husband.

"How do you put up with her?" Meg laughed, although I knew the remark had pissed her off. She only laughed to make me think she was a different person—not the one who bitched behind the back of every living creature, then to their face made them think she was the good guy, smoothing over their complaints and stroking their egos.

Cal interrupted us by escorting a student's mother, who was in a huff, to the door and saying the woman would like to meet with me. I broke off my conversation with Meg so I could deal with her.

She was small and blond, with freshly painted nails, a big diamond ring, and wearing shorts, sling sandals, and a T-shirt. She quickly told me she didn't have a lot of time to spend with me, because she was late for Pilates. I wanted to say, "Fine. Go sit on a rubber ball. I didn't call this meeting, so if you have no time for me, good-bye!" All of which is why Megan, and now Cal, handled the mothers. The young woman said she felt she needed to "get something across" to me, which implied we'd had this discussion before and I was simply too dense to understand whatever she was having to reiterate, when in fact I'd never met with the woman. She ignored Meg, probably assuming that she worked for me.

"My daughter has her lessons in the arena twice a week, and has for over a year. She takes a lesson and then rides for an hour. But her time has been cut back to favor the daughter of a lesbian couple." I quickly corrected her, saying that wasn't true.

"If Cal needs the arena for the next lesson, she may have to ask a student to work at the far end, so they can both share, because unfortunately we don't have two indoor arenas. But I can assure you that a client's sexual orientation, religion, or political views don't have any impact on who gets to use the arena." As evidenced by the fact that I haven't yet kicked your cute little ass out altogether for being such a prejudiced, shallow little shit, I thought.

"A lot of your new clients are talking about the fact that you favor people when it comes to lessons and arena time." My mind immediately flashed on Margaret Windom. Was this part of her sabotage activity, as Mrs. Remington had warned me?

"Are you trying to say we favor people like me?" I asked evenly.

"They are just saying you may be, you know—"

"Lesbian? I guess you missed the party announcement. Yes. I'm definitely a lesbian. If you're prejudiced against lesbians, I understand, and I'd like to give you a full month's refund so you can find a riding school run by right-wing tele-evangelists who pray before they get on their horses. And the way most of them ride, they should pray." The woman looked stunned, whirled, and hurried out the door. Cal, who'd caught the entire conversation, stepped back into the office and closed the door. "How many do you intend to fire?"

Megan burst out laughing. "Oh my God, Rae. You're worse than you used to be. Why don't you just post a sign out front: *Lesbian Riding Academy: Stay Out!*" All three of us laughed for the first time, and for just a second we were no longer enemies, just women trying to make it all work.

"And who's the lesbian couple bringing their daughter here to ride? News to me." I stared at Cal.

"No idea," Cal said, "but the mom who was just here obviously thinks she spotted one."

"I'm not putting up this façade any longer. A bunch of hypocrites. Gasp over the word 'damn,' then drug and rape people. Jane was right. I'm not giving up the good things in my life for the hypocrisy of theirs."

"I think I missed a beat—who got drugged and raped?" Megan's face scrunched up, but I ignored her question.

"Adios, Meg-alita," I said in reference to her seemingly ubiquitous serape. "We've got work to do here."

Meg leaned in and tried to kiss me good-bye, but I stepped back. "I'm with someone else. I'm off the market."

"Wow. Well, congratulations. I'm sure it's the woman that

was salivating over you the last time I was here. What's her name next door—"

"Good-bye, Meg," Cal said, and she walked off.

"One favor." Meg gave me a pleading look. "My mom's in the hospital, and she's not doing real well. I have to go up there tonight and see her."

"I'm sorry," I said, remembering her mom as a heavy-set woman who struggled with heart trouble and diabetes.

"I won't get out until about ten, when my dad comes up to stay with her. But I just can't go back to their house and spend the night alone. You know it's a big, creepy house to begin with, even if they're there, but I just don't want to…can I just spend the night here? I won't bother you."

"Go stay with your sister."

"Her kids are sick, and I don't want to expose my mom to more germs."

"Stay with a friend…rent a hotel room."

"I'll be in the spare bedroom. You'll never even see me. It's one overnight. Why are you being so mean?"

I let out a sigh, then said, "This will be the one and only time, Megan."

She thanked me, I gave her a new gate code, and she drove off.

Cal came back the minute she left, to make sure she had. "You do need a partner. She's right about that. Speaking of Jane, which we weren't, I know you two would be great business partners, if you didn't kill each other. She's a nice solid balance to your fire."

"Which is just your cowgirl-polite way of saying I fly off the handle and need stabilizing. I only said I was 'with someone' to get rid of Meg, not because I'm actually with someone."

"I understand," Cal said, and kept her poker face.

"So where is the great stabilizer these days?"

"Austin," Cal said too readily. "And it's perfect timing because I'm supposed to deliver this to you personally." Cal forked over a large, fancy envelope. I ripped it open, and inside was an invitation to a big rodeo and cutting-horse event to benefit child abuse. The event was this weekend in Austin, and the sponsor was Texas Bronc Riders to End Abuse. The association was sponsoring a two-day event, and the special guests included Jane Barrow. Before I could even react, I heard footsteps on the porch at the office door, and Margaret Windom was there, all bright-eyed and eager to tell me about her invitation to the Texas Bronc Riders benefit.

"Hello, ladies!" she boomed to both of us, obviously feeling she had the run of the place since she'd become our benefactor. "Perfect timing! My husband and I are planning to attend the benefit rodeo this weekend, and the benefactors' bronc party. We're taking our private jet and wanted to have you join us, Rae. Half a dozen other guests are headed that way."

"Thanks, Margaret, but no." I glared at her, and Cal quickly interceded.

"She's flying commercial with Wiley."

I looked surprised, and Margaret looked miffed, then tried again. "Well, maybe we can include Wiley on the plane."

"He's got lots of equipment, and an entourage, so his plans are made. I'll let him know you were kind enough to offer," Cal said firmly.

Margaret Windom didn't bother to hide her disgruntledness. She stomped off, slamming the door, and clomped down the office steps.

"Why did you tell her that?" I was irritated on many fronts.

"Because it's true. Here's your plane ticket. Jane asked that you please use it."

I tucked the ticket into my desk drawer. "Don't freak," I looked at Cal, "but Meg is coming back around ten thirty p.m. to spend the night. Her mom's in the hospital, and she's going there, and she doesn't want to spend the night alone in her parents' big house."

"Oh, brother! Well, her parents aren't going to get any younger, or any healthier, and their old house isn't going to get any smaller, or less creepy, so is she going to have to hide under the covers over here forever? That's probably just a big damned story she made up to get back in over here. Don't forget what she did to you."

"I thought you just lectured me on trusting people more, so I wouldn't be alone."

"I don't want you alone with Megan, and you can't trust her, that's for sure. She plays on your sympathy."

"Not going to happen."

"That's what you said about Margaret Windom," she said, and I could tell from her grimace, and the way she ducked her head, that she wished she hadn't said it.

❖

It was midnight when someone tapped at my bedroom door. I was startled until I remembered Meg had come in earlier, and was staying in the house, and was now already violating her "you'll never even see me" promise. I got up and cracked the door. She was in her nightshirt.

"My mom looked terrible," she said. "Can I come in and talk?"

"We'll talk in the living room," I said, rubbing my eyes and running my hand through my hair. I wasn't letting her into my bedroom.

"I'm sorry. I know you leave early for Austin in the

morning." That was so like Megan, apologizing for keeping me up all night while she kept me up all night.

"I don't know what to do." She started whimpering.

"To do about what?" I asked.

"My mother's ill, my dad can't handle it, and I have to move back from Massachusetts and live in their home and find a way to support myself. I don't know what to do."

"You do what you just said: help your parents, move back, get a job. It's called life."

"You can say that because you're already set up," she said.

"You left me in one big, fucking mess, and I figured it out. Now you have to do the same."

"Cal said you were going out of town. Can I stay here while you're gone? My mom should be out of the hospital by then."

"Damn it, Meg. This kind of—"

"I would do it for you."

I sighed. "When I get back, you have to be out of here. And stay out of Cal's way while I'm gone."

She nodded. That would probably mean a fight when I returned, but for now all I could think about was getting to sleep, and then getting to Austin.

CHAPTER TWENTY-TWO

On the plane ride to Austin, I became more and more nervous about being anywhere near the Windoms, particularly in a resort where I was unfamiliar with the surroundings.

"I don't understand how the Windoms got an invitation," I said to Wiley, who was jammed into the seat next to me, making me feel crowded but secure.

"JB saw to it," Wiley said. "I gotta tell you, Rae, JB's fury over the Windom people is at volcanic proportions."

"She's so mad she invited them to this event? That makes no damned sense."

"Jane's always thinkin'. And I can tell you, most of the time, lately, she's thinkin' about you." I could see in his eyes that the teasing was about to commence. "I mean you're a nice-lookin' gal, and all that, but I just don't get how you can cause weight loss, sleep deprivation, and no small degree of irritation in a strong woman like JB. You must have something I don't get." He gave me a grin.

"And you *won't* get it," I shot back. "Cuz I'm savin' it for JB."

Wiley giggled like a girl. Then he put his headset on and went to sleep, which I felt was an effort to avoid having to answer any questions about Jane.

We rode in the cab together from the airport to Palacio de los Caballos, a huge resort with three guest-room towers, multiple restaurants serving cuisine from a dozen different countries, and shopping that included everything from cowboy cabana-wear to diamond ankle bracelets in the shape of reins, everything in keeping with the hotel's name—the palace of horses. The resort featured multiple ballrooms and a coliseum-sized performance arena, attached to the north end. Wiley split immediately to find out if the equipment was set up correctly for Jane and to check on how Dark Horse had fared on the road trip. Jane's road crew had driven the famous gelding into town a day early, to rest up before he had to meet his admirers.

I checked in at the resort's front desk and then went to the ballroom, where Wiley said he'd be. The center of the ballroom had been turned into a small dirt arena, where a single horse could be ridden right up next to the tables. There were multiple bars, a massive sound system, wall-to-wall screens for showing videos on child abuse, and a lot of people checking out all the various audio and video systems. Apparently videos of Jane in her championship cutting events would be shown on the big screens all around the ballroom, and then the announcer would introduce her, and she would just ride into the tiny arena on Dark Horse and greet the crowd, pose for photos with the sponsors, and autograph anything they requested. So she was a "meet and greet" at this venue.

According to Wiley, the night flowed from a large public event in the massive arena, where Jane and others would show off their cutting-horse skills, then move to this ballroom, where several hundred invited guests would head for the photo op with Jane and Dark Horse, and finally those who signed up for the bronc busting would compete around midnight, in an area set up for the competition at one end of the ballroom.

Suddenly behind me, I heard her voice. "Ms. Starr, are you looking for someone?"

I whirled and threw myself at her, and she laughed as she hugged me.

"What is it about you?" I said, so glad to see her.

"I'm imprinted on you like a baby duck. No undoing it. I cleared my afternoon, so let's go to my room and freshen up."

"I don't think that's why you want me in your room," I said in a whisper.

We rode up in the elevator with several other guests, and one of the men wished her good luck tonight. She thanked him as we got off on the twenty-second floor, and I wondered if people could read the energy between us and know what we were up to. Jane touched her thumb to the door lock, and the sensor recognized her and let us in. The suite of rooms had a king-size bed and a beautiful view of Austin. But we weren't interested in the view and drew the heavy gold drapes.

"Do you ever worry that these hotels have cameras and people are watching us?" I asked.

"If they're watching, they're jealous that I have you in my room." Jane was through with speculative conversation and walked me backward toward the bed, then put her hands on my waist, lifted me, and tossed me back onto the bed.

"My God, you're strong," I said.

"I am." She smiled and raised one eyebrow playfully.

"You're going to perform in a few hours. Aren't you supposed to stay in training—no liquor and no sex?"

"In this case, it'll only make me better," she said, and crawled on top of me, shimmying my jeans down and unsnapping my bra to get to all the warm places she wanted to traverse.

"Have you made love in trucks for so long that you don't realize we could actually stand up and take our clothes off?"

"I think this is kind of sexy," she said, and I couldn't argue with that. "Okay, the boots." She surrendered, and I jumped up and kicked them off and stripped.

"That's even sexier," she said, and was out of her clothes in seconds. We got into bed, and she wrapped herself around me, pulling me into her with my back up against her chest, and her larger body made me feel like a small, protected animal, taking shelter inside her. She reached around my belly and began stroking me, making me push back against her until I couldn't take it any longer and flipped around to face her, demanding that she take me before I left my body. She gave me the Barrow grin and said it would be her pleasure, whereupon she was inside me, and I became entirely hers, giving myself to her in any way, as many times as she wanted me. My sexual surrender seemed to heighten her desire, and soon I was in her, making up for my smaller size with an intensity and passion I didn't even know I possessed. I could bring Jane Barrow to climax again and again, and that was thrilling.

"You could fucking kill me," she gasped.

"No. I want to keep you around," I said, and went down on her, and she moaned with pleasure and later fell asleep in my arms. I was physically exhausted after our nonstop, gymnastic lovemaking, but mentally energized just staring at Jane while she slept. She was so beautiful lying there, and I wondered what it might be like to wake up every morning with her beside me and go to bed every night curled up next to her body. But then my practical side kicked in. She said she couldn't cook, so would she think I was going to cook for her, and bring her coffee in bed? Maybe the age difference would make her decide she could order me around. She might be impossible and demanding once we were sharing the same pillows. Would she expect me to take her fancy clothes to the dry cleaners? Those were the kinds of things you didn't contemplate in the midst of lust. The alarm went off on her wristwatch, like a warning bell, and I jumped. She opened her eyes.

"Were you watching me sleep?" she asked sleepily.

"I was," I replied softly.

"And knowing you, you were cooking up a whole bunch of reasons why waking up with me might be problematic."

"Never," I lied, wondering if she suspected I was lying. She seemed to know things without being told sometimes, at least what horses were thinking, for sure.

We had to get dressed to show up at the arena for the cutting-horse competition. I couldn't imagine where she got the stamina, but she showered and blew her hair dry as I stood in the doorway and watched her. There was something so elegant about her, yet so masculine.

"What are you looking at?" she asked.

"At how the star puts herself together."

"You're sure you're in love with me and not the glitz?" she asked in a teasing fashion, but I felt, deep down, she wasn't teasing.

"Who said I was in love with you?" I said, smiling at her.

She threw a towel at me, and I ducked, and then she chased me back onto the bed, straddling me like a horse and holding me in place. "Are you in love with me?"

I stopped teasing and said quietly, "I'm afraid I am."

She kissed me, and I could see a difference in her eyes, like she'd relaxed. "I'm in love with you too." We didn't talk after that. It was like we both had to think about what we'd just said—what we'd committed to.

Fifteen minutes later, she was standing in front of me in a leather shirt covered in bling, with bling on her belt buckle and hat band. She had two faux diamond bands on her wrists. "The wrist bling is really turning me on," I said, and she kissed me again.

"Come on. I've got to go kiss my horse and get ready to do something spectacular," she said. We kissed again at the door before leaving the room, and I told her she looked great, and she was going to be great.

"My legs are shaking." She grinned. "Good thing Dark Horse knows what to do."

I goaded her. "I'm sure he's had to take over before in similar circumstances."

"No, he has not," she assured me as we rode down in the elevator and walked through the ballroom, winding around corridors, arriving at the huge public arena. She showed me where to sit—in a special booth for guests of the competitors. Now in public, with all the conservative cowboys around, I could only kiss her on the cheek, which didn't seem fair. She disappeared to get ready. When she left me, it was always like the lights had been turned off and I waited only for the next time I could see her.

The event was very similar to the big charity event she'd ridden in the first time I saw her on Dark Horse. At least two thousand people filled the stands, maybe more, all to see a big cutting-horse competition staged for a worthwhile cause. I bought something to drink, picked up a program, and settled in. It was getting close to time for the event to start when, out of nowhere, Wiley appeared.

"Dark Horse has pulled up lame. Wasn't that way this morning. Don't know what happened. Jane doesn't want to let anyone down, so she's going to ride another horse."

"She brought another horse?"

"No. Someone's going to loan her this hotshot mare to

ride tonight. She's determined not to disappoint the charity or the fans."

"Does she know the horse?" I was getting concerned.

"She's getting to know her right now. I'm a little worried myself. I hear she's a pretty difficult mare. Talented but difficult. Owner thinks everything will be okay, but the mare left her last rider in the dirt. He just couldn't keep up with her. But then Jane does pretty well with mares." Wiley joked nervously, and headed off to be with Jane, as I said a little too loudly, "In the dirt isn't good!"

It was one thing to be on a horse you knew, and had worked with for years, and you could trust. It was another to get on the back of a difficult mare you'd just met and ride out into the noise, and bright lights, and cattle, on the promise of the owner that he thinks everything will be okay. I wanted to go see Jane, but that would only distract her and maybe make her nervous, so I just looked up at the ceiling and said a prayer that she would, indeed, be okay. My mind flashed on Jane teasing me about her legs being shaky after our lovemaking, and I wondered how much "leg" a hotshot cutting horse required.

The announcer welcomed the guests and told them what a terrific night it was going to be, and how their price of admission went toward the fight against child abuse. Then he made all the housekeeping announcements—thanking sponsors and volunteers, and explaining the rules for the novices in the audience, as my heart beat faster than usual, and my breathing became erratic. Finally, he said, he had one announcement to make. Dark Horse had suffered a leg injury in transport and couldn't be ridden. The crowd gasped and then moaned in disappointment. The announcer quickly gave them "the good-news sandwich."

"Jane Barrow will ride for the charity on another horse,

Hedy Lamarr." Older people in the crowd laughed at the horse being named after an outspoken, old-time movie actress. "Ms. Barrow just met Ms. Lamarr this afternoon, so let's see if the two ladies get along." Everyone applauded.

Jane was first up, and I could see her at the end of the arena, outside the gates, astride a tall palomino mare who was tossing her head, stomping around, and dancing sideways as if she wanted to be anywhere but under Jane Barrow. I wasn't a cutting-horse expert, but it looked to me like Hedy Lamarr was a little fresh and could have used another forty-five minutes in the loping ring, but then her owner probably didn't even intend for her to be ridden tonight, so she might have had no warmup at all.

The announcer introduced them: "Hedy Lamarr, owned by Dream Girl Stables and ridden by Jane Barrow." The gates swung open, the crowd applauded, and Jane touched her hand to her hat, acknowledging the audience. She wasted no time riding Hedy Lamarr into the herd of cattle. I could tell from the square of her shoulders that Jane was relaxed, even though she wasn't on Dark Horse, but I did wonder if she felt like she'd traded in her recliner for a Shaker straight-back. She was on top of the mare's every move, subtly guiding and encouraging her with her posture and position, and the golden mare responded, suddenly becoming all business, slipping deep into the center, and practically hypnotizing the baldy directly in front of her. Hedy was face up with the steer, pulling him forward and out. Jane dropped the reins, signaling to Hedy that she'd committed, and Hedy Lamarr became a star, her big palomino body swinging right, then left as the steer made a break for it, but the big mare launched like a Learjet, her blond mane and tail flying through the air. The steer broke and ran again, but the mare was quicker and out-thought him, making a dramatic three-sixty spin in front of him that stunned all of us and froze the animal. It was an unexpected, flashy dash that I don't think even Jane anticipated. The crowd loved it. I could see Jane grinning even from my seat in the stands. The steer backed up, Jane signaled Hedy to quit the cow and picked up the reins, as the crowd roared, and the announcer intoned, "Well, now, that's how you ride a mare you never met! The incomparable Jane Barrow on Miss Hedy Lamarr, ladies and gentlemen." It was over, and the crowd was on its feet. This time I joined the groupies out back of the arena, along with the owner of Hedy Lamarr.

"You ever want to sell this mare," Jane patted her, "let me know."

"Well, you two sure looked good together," the fellow who owned her said.

"You were stunning." I hugged her, not caring if anyone heard the love in my tone of voice. She held out her bejeweled arm and draped it over my shoulder, holding me next to her as she answered questions and signed autographs. I realized I was under her wing like all the other women pictured in the internet articles, but I pushed that image out of my mind. Jane chatted, and laughed, and charmed her way through thirty minutes of fandom before we moved on to part two of the evening's activities—the meet-and-greet in the ballroom. On the way over, I asked her what riding Hedy Lamarr was like.

"Kind of like dating you. Gorgeous, opinionated, difficult, almost uncontrollable, but if you give her the right signals, it's magic. And my legs are killing me!"

I laughed, too impressed with her to be difficult tonight. She had pulled off a fantastic performance. "How will we know who won?" I asked, regarding the competition.

"I rode a difficult mare I'd never met, who didn't leave me in the dirt, and we had the crowd on their feet. I won," she said, and we both laughed.

In the time we'd been in the arena, the ballroom had been transformed. One end of the room was tricked out to look like a barn, with a lot behind it, where a techno-bronc was standing frozen, waiting for the contestants and technical instructions. People had already begun to gather, getting a drink from the bar and signing up on the bronc-riding sheet for a chance to win ten grand in cash, if they could stay on the electronic bronc for eight seconds.

A couple of people who wanted Jane to autograph something intercepted her. One kid even asked her to sign his arm. "Now if you don't ever intend to wash that arm again, don't date any women I know." Her remark made him laugh and blush.

We hadn't been there twenty minutes when Margaret and Steve Windom surfaced, racing over to join us. Margaret showed no signs of remorse after my unloading on her, or concern that I might shoot one or both of them. Apparently, they felt their money made them bulletproof.

"You were amazing!" Margaret Windom crooned, and Jane thanked her.

"Impressive!" Steve Windom chimed in.

"So lovely of you to make our room special." Margaret swooned again at Jane. "The front desk said you'd left the wine, and flowers, and fruit. Serendipitous!"

"We appreciate our big donors," Jane said, and my shoulders locked up.

"Are you riding in here as well?" Margaret was so admiring of Jane that I wanted to slap her. *And where would she ride in a space the size of a tiny dance floor? Does she think we're going to let loose a herd of cattle in between the cocktail tables?*

"Just saying hello, being supportive. You riding the techno-bronc, Steve?" Jane addressed Mr. Windom as if they socialized together.

He laughed. "Well, if I did that, I'd have to stop drinking right now."

"If you'll excuse us, I want to introduce Rae to a former sponsor of mine." Jane dragged me off toward the stage.

"Just breathe," she said, correctly reading my body language and sensing that conversation with the Windoms was about to send me over the deck. "It's going to be a great evening."

The man up on the stage was the cowboy version of Colonel Sanders. He greeted Jane, and she quickly introduced me, saying this was Butch Butterfield, a longtime friend. He asked if she was ready to get started, and she told him to give her a minute to get Dark Horse. Jane excused herself and walked out back of the ballroom, where I could see that her team had Dark Horse waiting, tacked up and curried, his leg wrapped in a glitzy, spangled material that made it look less like a bandage and more like part of his tack. Butch Butterfield waited for her signal, and then someone threw a spotlight on the entrance where she stood with her horse, and the band played a musical intro as Butterfield said, "Ladies and gentlemen, Dark Horse is ready to join the party! You'll notice he's partied too hearty and has his leg wrapped, so his owner Jane Barrow won't be riding him, but he will pose for pictures in appreciation of your kind donations to this cause."

Jane gently walked Dark Horse into the ring, people applauded, and he looked majestic, as if he knew what his job was and was going to make sure everyone understood, wrapped leg or not, that he was a champion. He let the guests stroke him, and talk to him, and attendees asked Jane questions. She signed autographs and posed for pictures with the donors, and Dark Horse looked happy.

I appreciated that she put his health and well-being ahead of her ego. She didn't try to ride him in or even sit on him. She just stood beside him and gave him a pat on the neck. Then after a half hour or so, she led Dark Horse back out of the tiny arena, and a young, dark-haired woman took his lead and led him back out of sight. Jane Barrow was a kind woman.

CHAPTER TWENTY-THREE

Jane joined me at the foot of the stage and explained that
Butch Butterfield was hosting the benefactors' bronc party,
so I figured he was a fairly wealthy guy. The old, white-hair,
paunchy oilman-rancher seemed fond of Jane; at least the two
of them were on back-slapping terms, sharing jokes I wasn't
in on.

"Butch reached out to all the wealthy donors personally
and put the screws to them, to make sure they showed up,"
Jane said, and I assumed the Windoms had gotten screwed by
Butch—an ironic reversal—because they were certainly front
and center.

"I'm trying to get Jane, here, to sign up for bronc riding,"
he said to me, "but she's too smart. Now these men, they'll do
anything. May talk Steve Windom into it, before the night's
over." He laughed. "The sheer weight of his ego should hold
his ass in the saddle, wouldn't you say, JB?" She laughed and
waved him off, as if unwilling to participate in his benefactor-
bashing.

Jane guided me over to the auction items and said sotto
voce, "Butch isn't a Windom fan. Thinks Steve Windom got
the best of him in an oil deal."

"Did he?" I was curious.

"Not enough that it hurt his pocketbook, but enough that it hurt his pride. And in Texas, men ride for pride."

People moved around the floor looking at auction items and getting drinks from the bar. Butch, who obviously enjoyed double duty as the announcer, picked up the mic, and in a big, booming voice reminded the men to put their names on the sign-up sheet, and "Autograph that little waiver form, releasing us from any claim of injury. If you and that electronic bronc don't get along, tell it to your chiropractor. We don't want to hear about it. And remember, it's okay to change your mind at the last minute if you're too knee-walkin' drunk to ride, and we'll mark your name off. But you can't come in late and sign up. So sign up now. You'll be judged on if you stay on the bronc for eight seconds, and how high you crank the motor up."

All the young guys were writing their names down, and Jane spent too much time chatting up Steve and Margaret Windom, as far as I was concerned. It was like she'd become their best bud, which didn't make me feel good, after what they'd done to me. It was hard for me to even think the words "what they'd done to me." Most of the time when I thought about it, I used the phrase "after what had happened to me," making it seem like it was an accident—like a tornado or flood or car wreck—rather than an attack by two people I could identify. "What happened to me" allowed me to disassociate. And with my attackers in the same room with me again, I wanted to leave my body. Steve and Margaret Windom's presence was forcing me to consider that other phrase: "what they'd done to me."

"Look at those crazy women swooning over every baby-faced boy who signs up. Half of them will be too drunk to ride by the time the competition starts." Jane paused and took a drink of her bourbon and Coke, and the overhead lights bounced off her wrist bling, turning her into Wonder Woman.

What was she up to? I could tell it was something.

Mr. Windom kept his eye on the boys signing up.

"This is a young man's game," Jane said. "Gotta be able to 'get it up' to even think about bronc-riding. That young stud over there looks like he could go for eight." She gestured toward a good-looking, buffed kid with two young girls snuggled up to him.

"It's not just youth. It's talent." Mr. Windom took a slug of his beer.

"I wouldn't risk it. Not even for all those good-looking babes who want to ride the guy who rode the bronc." She laughed.

"Now, Jane, are you trying to get me to sign up?" Mr. Windom asked, apparently aware she was taunting him with the prospect of young women who wanted celebrity sex.

"Of course I am. Look at the crazy thing I just did on a mare I'd never ridden. But I do respect a man who knows when he has to hang it up."

Steve Windom laughed and ambled off, and I saw him sidle up to the sign-up sheet, then pause, apparently trying to decide if he should add his name to the contestants.

Margaret Windom spotted him, and they had an animated conversation, but I couldn't tell whether she wanted him to ride or was trying to talk him out of it. I noticed Jane caught Butch Butterfield's eye and nodded toward the Windoms. Butch picked up the mic and drew everyone's attention to Steve Windom, standing at the sign-up table.

"Well, well, well. The competition is just about to get richer. The bronc-riding champ of California Polytechnic University is thinking about putting his name on the ledger.

Will he do it? Will one of the association's biggest benefactors be a contestant? Aaaaaand…" Butch dragged the word out to match the drag of the pen Steve Windom was signing up with. "He did it, folks! Steve Windom is going to ride. You young bucks might have just said good-bye to ten grand."

Steve Windom looked appropriately embarrassed, but he was hooked now. In for eight.

The party was lavish, Texas style, with a live auction, open bars, cowboy line dancing, and prizes for doing almost anything. It was like any other big Texas charity benefit, with a few additional party tricks: cocktail waitresses that looked like faux-bunnies, their huge breasts threatening to dive out of their skinny tops, and women on stilts wearing nothing but a G-string, moving awkwardly in and out of the crowd singing "The Eyes of Texas Are Upon You." Then there was the Cirque du Soleil trapeze equipment overhead, where performers swung, and dove, and caught one another over the heads of the partygoers, with nothing but a net between them and the donors.

After a couple of hours of raking in hundreds of thousands of dollars, the main event was announced—the bronc-riding contest. By now people were taking their seats at the cocktail tables surrounding the bronc paddock, some so drunk they were publicly groping one another. There was a barn façade like a flat on an old movie lot, and Butch was standing on its fake barn porch overlooking the action. He had the mic and got everyone's attention, thanked the benefactors, read the rules to the contestants, and had a pretend-priest come out and bless the electronic bronc as church bells tolled and people laughed.

"You mount the bronc and signal me to turn on the juice. We control direction, dips, twists, and turns. You get to control speed. You can keep it down low, or you can turn it up high.

Do it yourself, or," he jerked his thumb in the air, "give me the signal, and I'll crank it up for you remotely."

The bells tolled again in a mock requiem to sudden death, and the event began. Butch preceded each contestant with their name, where they were from, and their bronc-riding experience, if any. The first kid up looked skinny and scared. He was a local boy with no formal bronc-busting training, but he stayed on eight seconds, albeit a slow eight. Butch intoned, "Now there's a man who's set the bar. Only way you're going to beat him is to crank up the kick-ass on that bronc."

A few young boys took their turns. Out of ten contestants, three stayed on for the full eight, but no one had it cranked up very high. Then it was Steve Windom's turn. The crowd provided plenty of applause and reassurance that he could "do this" as the former college star straddled the bronc. Butch bellowed into the mic, "Mr. Steve Windom, Bronc Riding Champion of California Polytechnic University, and one of our top sponsors in the event tonight. Let her rip, Steve!"

Steve Windom signaled the remote controller, and the bronc bucked. Windom held on for three seconds, as people shouted encouragement, and then he signaled Butch to crank it up, but I don't think he realized how far "up" was, and seven seconds in, Steve Windom went out the back door, flying off the rear end of the techno-bronc, and he never got up. Jane didn't move, saying only, "Wiley, see if you can give him a hand." But no one could give him a hand, because he couldn't move, and one leg drifted up slightly into the air like it was tethered to nothing at all, signaling that Mr. Windom would not be bronc riding in the foreseeable future.

Margaret screamed. The announcer called for an ambulance, and Steve Windom was writhing in pain.

"Oh my God!" I shouted, and glanced at Jane, who

never looked at me. As Steve Windom was hauled out, Butch Butterfield kept rolling. "Ladies and gentlemen, a round of applause for one of our great benefactors, Steve Windom. We wish him well, and we'll provide you with an update when we have one. And now contestant number twelve, Jack Winchester." Young Jack Winchester rode the bronc at full throttle and took home ten thousand dollars. I suspected Mr. Windom wouldn't be home for quite a while.

I watched Jane afterward talking to the old announcer, and he laughed and patted her on the back. She rejoined me, and I was still pretty shook up.

"He could have been killed!" I said of Steve Windom.

"Got hurt worse than I expected," she said.

"You expected him to get hurt?"

"He told me at your party that he hadn't trained in thirty years, so of course I expected he'd get hurt."

"Someone said he may have broken his hip." I was fretting.

"I doubt that. But he sure won't be grabbing his crotch any time soon," she said into the air.

Jane, with the help of Butch Butterfield, had encouraged Steve Windom to ride. Was that her payback on my behalf, or just payback to all men who rape or compromise women? I knew it wasn't kind-hearted of me, but I saw cosmic retribution in what had happened to the man who'd participated in my degradation that frightening night at his home.

Wiley walked over. "That was one hell of a landing Windom took."

"He's lucky. Could have been worse," Jane said.

"Only if he'd died," I said.

Jane kind of shrugged, downed her drink, and didn't add to the conversation, making me think that growing up on the rodeo circuit must toughen a person.

❖

That night over a glass of wine on the patio, I told Jane I had a proposition for her. I'd been thinking about it ever since she'd asked me to travel with her. I'd thought about it again when Cal mentioned the fact that she thought Jane and I would be great partners. And then I thought about it again on the plane ride over. "I think we should combine our businesses, and our ranches. I want you to come home." I let my breath out, having said what I never thought I'd say to anyone. I'd just blurted it out without any preparation or buildup whatsoever. And frankly I felt stupid after I said it and wished I could go back and rephrase it. But Jane didn't seem to mind. And I could tell when I mentioned the word "home" that it had the desired effect. Jane had never really had one, and she ducked her head.

"Now that sounds a little bit like a personal proposal, not just a business proposition." She pulled herself together. "Why don't you come to my suite tonight, and we'll seal the deal." She took my hand.

Suddenly a woman my age, who looked just like the woman in the photo in the latest article from New Mexico, appeared on the patio and draped herself over Jane, introducing herself to me playfully as Sonny Brown.

"Has Jane shared our history together?" she asked, and Jane said she was just about to get to that. My heart rate increased. What hadn't she told me?

Sonny directed her comments to me. "I'm one of the gals who's part of her crew. I've traveled with her for going on twenty years, and I make sure she eats right, goes to bed early, and doesn't hang out with the wrong people. And as you can see, I've failed miserably."

"I think I spoke to you on the road," I said, and told her it was nice to meet her. She leaned over, gave Jane a big kiss on the cheek, and playfully punched her. "Don't get yourself in trouble now." Jane was obviously fond of her, because she'd chosen to travel with her for two decades, but the show of affection embarrassed her, if her red cheeks meant anything— embarrassed her like the woman at the casino had. It all felt like so many other times with Jane—things were going great, and then women swarmed in on her. Our relationship was new and exciting. What would happen if we were together for a while, and I was old hat, and young girls were throwing themselves at her?

My stomach turned, and I grew light-headed. I made an excuse to go to the bathroom, getting up and rushing past all the tables with their horse centerpieces, and confetti, and streamers. I pushed open the ladies' room door, rushed into a stall, and threw up. I felt weak, and like I was about to be taken advantage of again—if not now, then in the future, after I'd committed to putting our lives in a blender. I stared into the long mirror over the sinks and told myself I couldn't stay. I needed to leave right now and fly back to the ranch. *I keep getting sucked in. I have to break this cycle.*

I rushed to my room, gathered up my things, and texted Wiley I was leaving, and to tell Jane I was sorry I couldn't stay.

Wiley came skidding up to me as my bag was being loaded into a town car. "What happened?" He looked stunned.

"She's never going to settle down, and certainly not with me, Wiley. You were right."

"Shit," he said and grabbed his head with both hands, as I patted his shoulder and left.

Chapter Twenty-four

I was back at the ranch not even forty-eight hours after I'd left for Austin, and I was lost, really. All my thoughts and plans that had included Jane were now up in smoke. And to add to my depression, Meg was still camped out in my house.

Cal approached, having been left with her while I was gone. "Is she staying?" Her voice indicated she was clearly fed up. "Because if she is, I'm not. None of us are going to be ordered around by the Diva Dumpling, which is what she's trying to do again."

"No," I said. "She's not staying. She said her mother was—"

"So Ellie and I are moving her out."

"I'll do that," I said, trying not to shirk my responsibility. I walked into the house calling Meg's name. She appeared in sweats, with her iPad, as if she were vacationing somewhere. "Meg, I told you, you'd have to leave when I returned."

"I'll be gone in the morning—"

I took a deep breath. "Sorry, Meg, but it's gotta be now."

"Your staff continues to run the show, I see." Meg huffed off in the direction of her room. Minutes later, Ellie made three trips to Meg's car, carrying out bags and other items.

"Where did all this stuff come from?" I asked Cal.

"She started moving in the moment you left, and now she's moving out," Cal said, as Ellie escorted her to her car.

"Thanks, Cal," I said. It was all I could muster.

"You know, if Jane Barrow spent the night under the same roof with an ex-lover, let her have the run of her ranch for a few days, and then told you nothing was going on, you'd accuse her of lying and running around, and yet when you do it, it's nothing. Ever notice that?" she said, and stomped off. I didn't respond. Truth was truth.

❖

I wasn't much use. Cal kind of walked around me like I was furniture. And I just sat on the porch staring off into space. Hairy and Sally stayed by my side. The cool breeze teased us with the possibility of fall, and the barn swallows were leaving, signaling chilly weather ahead. But even that wonderful weather transition I'd waited for all summer couldn't bring me any joy.

Finally, one evening, Cal brought me a glass of wine and propped her feet up on the porch bench, leaning back in a rocker, and just sat there without saying a word. After about twenty minutes, I said, "What?"

"Nothing. Just stopped by to see if you were still breathing."

I ignored her remark. I hadn't told her anything about the event in Austin, or why I'd left. I assumed Wiley had filled her in on everything, but even he didn't know that I'd walked out because Jane seemed to enjoy having women hang on her, despite the fact she was with me.

"Gotta get back on the horse, Rae. Isn't that what we tell the kids when they fall off? Gotta get back on, no matter how scared you are to do it." She knocked off the wine and plunked her glass down.

"What horse are you referring to?" I asked snidely, expecting her to deliver a dissertation on Jane Barrow.

"Life. Live it, or give it up. Cuz I'm kind of tired of seeing your half-dead carcass laying around on the porch drawing flies," she said with dark humor and walked off.

After that, I got up off my ass. Sometimes you need someone to remind you it's time to put your own boot in your own butt. I walked over to the barn, having forgotten we had some of the veterans visiting today, working the horses. I spotted Mike. Dusty had apparently driven him out to the ranch. He waved to me, and it struck me how much more outgoing he was than when he first arrived. I walked up and hugged him, and he thanked me again, as he did every time for letting him "have a horse."

"You seem sad," he said, surprising me with his correct diagnosis, and more so that he would even notice.

"A little." I smiled at him. "But it will pass."

"You know what I do when I get sad?" he asked.

I shook my head no.

"I pet a horse." He took my hand and placed it on Snow's neck and pushed my palm down until I petted her. When I tried to stop, he said, "Keep petting her. She likes it." I tried to stop again, but he wouldn't let me. "Keep petting her." I had to laugh.

"When can I stop?" I asked.

"Ask her?" he said. I let my hand up, and she immediately punched me with her nose, telling me to continue. "Nope, not yet," he said, and we both laughed again. I felt lighter.

My phone rang, and I had to step away, which was probably a good thing, or God knows how long Mike would have insisted I pet Snow. I took a moment to thank him before taking the call.

The voice on the phone introduced himself as an attorney friend of Jane's. He said Jane had asked him to call me. He wanted to know if I was going to file suit against my attacker and issue a statement inviting others to come forward. I told him no. He said Jane had given him permission to talk about her experience along the lines of my mine.

"I was Jane's attorney thirty-five years ago when she was pregnant and didn't know what to do."

"Doesn't sound like you did her any favors, if she had to have the baby," I said coldly.

"Her grandmother raised Sonny and Jane both. Jane left home when she turned eighteen, but she kept in touch, and when Sonny turned eighteen, she started traveling with Jane. Anyway, Jane knows the kind of decisions a rape case entails, so she asked me to help."

I was stunned. *Sonny, the woman in Austin, was Jane's daughter.* My mind completely disengaged from the purpose of the attorney's call and got jammed on Sonny being Jane's child. I wanted to hang up and just live with that revelation for a moment, but the attorney was still on the line. "Are you there?" he asked.

That woman my age is her daughter. It's horrible that it's true, and it's horrible that I thought Jane was running around with her and didn't bother to ask who she was, or anything else that would have revealed Sonny was her child.

"I appreciate your calling. I just need some time to think about it," I murmured to her attorney.

"Most likely the Windoms have sexually assaulted other women. If their methodology is relatively smooth, that usually indicates they've done it before." He gave me his phone number, and we hung up.

I sat there thinking the Windoms were indeed pretty smooth. A business meeting, time spent discussing the program, conversation about her daughter and husband, a nice dinner, her assistant dismissed—the wine from the carafe before dinner must have been just wine, but the wine from the carafe poolside obviously spiked—sitting on the mats by the pool to look at the stars while the drug took effect. Everything was mapped out. All they needed each time was an idiot like me. *I was fortunate I didn't fall into the pool, because as immobilized as I was, I would definitely have drowned. I guess I can be grateful for that.*

Cal walked over, saying she had something she wanted to tell me about Wiley and her, but I unloaded first. "Did you know Sonny is Jane's daughter?"

Cal didn't say anything to make me feel better. "Jesus, Rae. You didn't know that?"

"I guess I'm not plugged into wireless-Wiley the way you are." I snorted, and she ignored the barb.

"You flew all that way, could have been in bed with her that night, and you spin and turn. Wiley called when you left, and he was so upset. The man thinks you're something special, but he can't stand it that you continue to hurt Jane."

"You and Wiley are like two teenage girls on the phone constantly gossiping."

"And you give us a lot to gossip about! Wiley called me from the hotel in Austin when you marched out, to say he thought you didn't understand that the thirty-five-year-old woman you were so freaking jealous of is Sonny Barrow Brown."

"I know that now," I said.

"You seem to know things a little too late, wouldn't you say?"

I didn't respond. Even though she worked for me, Cal was like family, and lately she was the family I wanted to desert.

"Brown was the father, and Jane kept Sonny, and she's a great kid. And a hell of a horsewoman, according to Wiley. You always run before you have all the information, because you're so afraid you might find a reason to stay. Jane Barrow is a good woman. But maybe you need another lover like your last one, just so you can be miserable."

"In case you forgot, she's the one who ran off!" I said of Megan.

"Me too," she said, and ran off before I could say anything more.

As soon as she was out the door, I called the attorney back and told him he'd have to take the case pro bono, with no guarantee of any money unless I won. He said he was in New Mexico, so he'd draw up our agreement, and then we'd file in Oklahoma. After that, his partner here would probably come out to the ranch to meet me.

I slid back into angst—envisioning front-page stories about one of the city's biggest philanthropist couples being targeted as sex perverts, the lesbian label being applied not only to me but any woman on the ranch, the loss of grant money due to the bad press, and certainly no Jane Barrow after my once again showing her I didn't trust her. The only things I would get out of this were retribution and a clean slate.

Later that afternoon, I called Cal and Ellie into the office and apologized for being so moody and difficult. Apologizing seemed to be all I did lately. I told them I wanted to explain in more detail what had happened at the Windom Estate, and I walked them through the entire evening right up until dawn, when the car was waiting for me. Ellie's eyes were bugged out like a bullfrog, but she remained quiet. Mine was quite a story for a young girl to absorb. I told them in detail what Margaret and her husband had done to me, while I was unable to move, and I saw tears gather in Cal's eyes, but she held them back.

"I'd like to go over there and beat the bejesus out of that woman," Ellie said, with the energy of youth, wanting to take the most direct route to justice.

"Thank you, Ellie, but I'm going to bring charges. I just spoke to an attorney today. That could mean all kinds of retaliation from the Windoms, and it will undoubtedly cause issues with clients, the press, and any and everybody else, so I don't want you to feel overwhelmed when all that starts. And if you can't take it, well, I understand," I said, leaving them room to quit if they needed to. I asked that they not talk about the case and, if anyone talked to them, refer them to me. They both nodded, and that was that.

Then, that evening, I met with Dusty Daniels, who ran the veterans' program. She staggered up the wooden steps to my office, her big handbag banging against her ample thigh, and I'd come to appreciate her frowsy appearance for what it was—too busy making things happen for others to worry about what might happen for her.

I came right out and told her I'd been attacked, and was filing charges, and unfortunately her program was in the middle of all this. "I doubt the Windoms will try to get their money back for the first year of funding, because that would look punitive. Allowing the program to run under their name makes them look like beneficent people. But when the year is up, I have no idea where funding will come from." I offered to let her end the program with my ranch, but Dusty refused, saying she knew me to be a good woman, and she would stand by me. Her support was touching and made me tear up. And frankly, I was tired of tears. We hugged good-bye and determined, for the moment, to continue to run the program just as we were doing, until we knew how things were going to shake out.

"I can tell you one thing," Dusty said. "Those old vets could care less about any of this hoopla. They're just grateful to be out here with the horses. So my goal is to continue to make that happen and to look for other donors to support the program." She patted me on the arm, then took hold of the porch railing and walked down the steps, huffing and puffing slightly from the exertion. "Lot of bad things happen to us women. But we're kinda like Johnson grass—tough, tenacious, and damned hard to kill. So you just hang in there." She climbed into her old Pontiac and drove away, and I liked Dusty Daniels even more.

It had been a stressful day reliving that night at the Windom mansion, and I was tired, so I poured myself a drink and pulled up a chair on the south porch off the office about the time Wiley came over to visit. I didn't know he was back from Austin, and I was glad to see him. I poured him a drink too, and he put his boots up on the porch and tilted his hat back, acting like he was staying awhile. He was a slow talker when the talk was serious, so I settled in.

"Want to first off say thank you for the advice you gave me about my wife. She signed the papers, and the divorce is final."

"Great news," I said flatly, unable to put much emphasis into my reaction.

"I proposed to Cal, and she said yes." He beamed.

I did smile over that. "She didn't tell me. Congratulations!"

"And we're going to live on the Barrow Ranch and do what we're doing now."

"Well, that's a relief," I said, and meant it.

"We'd like to have the ceremony here, if you don't mind. Our place is more cattle-y, and yours looks nicer for that kind of thing."

"I'd be real honored."

"And my last piece of news is that Jane drove in late last night, and she's coming over to see you in about thirty minutes." He giggled like a girl, and I turned into the Pointer Sisters—so excited, I couldn't hide it.

"Wiley, you ornery thing!"

"Hey, I had to get my news out first, because once you hear Jane's here, I might as well be a pile of cow poop. I'm leaving now!" He ducked as I tossed a porch cushion at him.

I ran inside to fix my hair and makeup, and put on a clean shirt, and got back out on the porch just as her big black SUV pulled in, this time with a horse trailer on the back I didn't recognize. She got out slowly and closed the door, then leaned back against the vehicle and just stared at me. I stood on the porch and leaned up against a porch post, staring back.

"You spook and run real easy," she said, and I ducked my head. "Here. I've got something." She walked to the back of the horse trailer and deftly unloaded a white horse with a big, thick mane and tail, who looked just shy of fourteen hands. She walked the beautiful animal over and handed me the lead rope.

"She's gorgeous," I said. "Who does she belong to?"

"She's an engagement gift."

"Cal will love her." I stroked the beautiful mare's nose, then put my arms around her neck, and she curved her head around me, protecting me like I was her foal. I thought she was wonderful and told Jane that.

"She's yours."

"*My* engagement gift?" I laughed.

"The only way I'm ever going to get you to settle down about me, and share a home with me, and quit disappearing on me, is to marry you."

"I'm not marrying you!" I said, completely shocked at the suggestion.

"Yes, you are. I'm putting you on notice. I generally get what I want. And I want you forever." Jane kissed me, and it was the kind of kiss that seals the deal. The kiss that said I was home, and owned, and in love, and loved, and would have roots and a family, even if it was just Wiley and Cal and Sonny.

Gesturing toward the horse, she gave me the Barrow grin. "Which of us do you want to ride first?" I cut her an amused look, then hugged the pony-sized white mare and whispered into her big, furry ear. "You were brought here by a gambler who thinks she's going to walk onto this ranch, and run the tables, and own us all." And then I gave Jane a searing look that said that would actually be fine with me.

Cal walked up, her mood changing to ebullient upon seeing Jane. "Well, welcome home!" She said the words like she was really excited about Jane's arrival, and they sounded right.

"Thank you, Cal. Would you mind taking Lady Luck to the barn for dinner, while I spend some time with Rae."

"Seems like there's two lucky ladies," Cal said.

"And congratulations on Wiley. You got yourself a good man," Jane added.

"Yes, you did, Cal." I locked eyes with her to let her know I was sorry I hadn't celebrated him earlier, and sorry about a lot of things.

Chapter Twenty-five

This time our lovemaking was different—slow, with an intense heat, and filled with a soft passion, as if we knew we could have each other forever and didn't have to cram everything into one night. I lay beside her, stroking every part of her, looking at the size of her hands compared to mine, putting my foot next to hers to see the difference in length, drawing my fingers down the creases next to her eyes and the line of her jaw—touching her as if I now owned her and wanted to see everything I'd bought. I could tell my unabashed appraisal amused her, because she said, "Anything you want to send back to the factory for repair?"

"Nope. Just want to take you in from top to bottom, because you're mine now."

"I was yours from the moment I met you. But I knew you'd be difficult to land, because you're so damned full of yourself."

"Which is why you're attracted to me," I replied.

"That and other things," and she made love to me. Her large, graceful hands cupped every part of me, slowly caressing and stroking me, then suddenly building to such an overwhelming intensity that I came immediately. Love with Jane Barrow could make me lose my mind. It disengaged all thought processes and connected me to some primal emotion that was all about touch and sensation. Would it wear off, would I ever find her touching me ordinary, or would this state of lust and longing always be resurrected whenever she reached for me?

After a while, we managed to pull ourselves together and walk out onto the porch, barefooted and dreamy-eyed, only to find Margaret Windom standing there, waiting for us. I was unpleasantly startled but made no attempt to conceal my love for Jane. I did, however, make a mental note to change Margaret's gate code.

"How's your husband?" Jane asked, and her tone was flat, like she was being polite but in truth could have cared less.

"He'll be recuperating for several months," she said. Jane just nodded pensively, like she was astro-traveling to have a look for herself. Then Margaret Windom turned her eyes to me, saying her attorney had warned her not to come near me, but she wanted to talk and asked if Jane could give her a few minutes. Jane looked at me to see what I wanted to do, and I nodded that she could let Margaret have a minute. Jane stood off to one side of the porch, but I was certain not out of earshot, because she didn't trust Margaret Windom. Nor did I.

"I told you I have issues with my medication—"

"That's bullshit," I snapped.

"My husband can't get an erection—"

"So you drug women, and rape them, to help him 'get off'? How many women besides me?" I was on the attack.

"I'm not here to discuss stats." Her tone was dismissive.

"Does your daughter know about this?" She glanced away rather than answer. "But she will. That's the sad part. I have no way to stop you, monitor you, or protect other women and girls unless I press charges."

"I could lose my child."

I saw her anguish, and it moved me. But her situation wasn't of my making. "I have to do something for my own sanity," I said.

Margaret was good at switching gears, and when her sympathy gambit didn't work, she resorted to a power play, saying over her shoulder as she walked down the porch steps, "You may be sorry if you do anything. Don't ever doubt that I can ruin you."

"You might want to ask your attorney if it's okay to threaten and intimidate the person you drugged and raped, or maybe you like doubling down on your crimes." I spoke loudly, and the volume seemed to shatter her façade. She fled to her car.

Jane stood beside me. "Don't let her get to you. She's the one in trouble, not you." But it didn't feel that way. I felt like I was in trouble as well—how could I not when so much was at stake—my reputation, my business, my integrity. Jane evidently saw me tense up and begin to fret. "I think you need someone to stay over and take your mind off Margaret Windom, and I'm just the woman who can do that." She led me back to the bedroom, and I curled up in her arms.

❖

The sun came up and Jane Barrow was in my bed, and for the first time she had nowhere to be but right here with me. I loved the feeling of waking up to her. We wrapped around one another like two small animals, the warmth of our bodies making us drift in and out of sleep. If she moved, I automatically adjusted my position to hold her, and if I moved she did the same.

"Let's stay here all day," she said, in a sleepy voice, and I agreed. But then the phone rang. It was Cal with a list of questions regarding preparations for her wedding. After five minutes of having to focus on wedding details, I finally sat up in bed.

"I'll make coffee," Jane moaned, and got up.

I covered the phone so Cal couldn't hear, and beamed at Jane. "You know how to do that?"

"You'd be surprised what I know how to do." She bounced back into bed, took the phone from me, and pretended she had accidentally disconnected Cal, giving me a mischievous grin. Then she dove on me and kissed me senseless, and we made love in the morning as the sun came through the windows and the moms and their charges came through the gates. I felt like I no longer had anything to hide. Jane Barrow had freed me.

The wedding preparations were a good diversion from endlessly thinking about Margaret Windom and how she had changed my life forever. The wedding was a happier kind of stress, and Cal behaved like a nervous teenager. Should there be a procession and a ringbearer, who should the minister be, and what should the invitations look like? Dawn till dusk Cal was just one big series of questions and issues, until I couldn't stand it anymore and asked permission to take over.

Since it was going to happen fast, we created an electronic invitation, featuring flowers and horses, and the bride and groom's photograph, and we got them out in forty-eight hours. The wedding would take place mid-morning, followed by a chuckwagon brunch with nice tables scattered throughout the lawn, and special plates, and silverware. A cowboy wedding band would play, and people could dance in the barn aisles. We'd have Ellie and her friends hang wedding lanterns and streamers, and Wiley would arrange for a surrey and horses to take the newlyweds around the property for pictures. Everyone got their assignments and embellished whatever they'd been asked to do, seemingly excited that the heat had finally subsided, and we had something joyful to celebrate.

❖

The wedding was right out of *Oklahoma*, with the surrey, and horses, and the porch rails all decorated, and Cal in a white gingham frock, and Wiley in a cowboy tux with a string tie. It was sweet, and beautiful, and I was so happy for them. Cal's students were there, and Wiley invited Belle. After all, she was part of his life too. The photographer took pictures of the newlyweds on horseback and standing beside the fence, where a few roses were still growing. Dark Horse and Howie made almost every photo, but the two white mares, Beauty and Snow, were in there too, having gained enough weight to make them look like big, white fairy-tale horses. Mike and John, wearing their old military uniforms, led them around, looking as proud as fathers of the bride. Dusty had driven them over, and she was now stationed at the punch bowl sucking down the vodka and cranberry, making me think Ellie might have to drive them all home.

The wind was blowing a cool breeze over the fifty or so guests, the intermittent storms had greened every pasture, and the entire place looked like a movie set. These moments made ranching all worthwhile. I stood next to Jane, my arm around her, feeling better than I had in years.

The minister was an uncle of Wiley's who flew in to marry the couple. He called everyone together in front of the prettiest view on the place, a small slope overlooking the horse barns, and pastures, and paddocks. He was an old-timey,

Bible-thumping man who, despite his slightly out-of-date three-piece suit and boots worn down at the heels, seemed to have a kind heart, a deep booming voice, and a playful nature.

Wiley and Cal took their places in front of him, and he said, "Marriage is about trust. Building it, earning it, and having it. Your wife or husband is the one person you should be able to trust at all times, about all things. If your trust is broken in a marriage, then you must repair it, because marriage is love, and love is built on many things, but among the most important is trust. Cal, I take it you trust this man…as far as you can throw him?" Cal looked shocked, and we all laughed. "I meant to say, Cal, do you trust this man enough to take him as your husband?" Cal said she did. "And Wiley, I take it you trust this woman with your life…because as we men all know, if you upset this woman, your life IS in her hands." The crowd laughed again. "Wiley, do you take this woman as your wife?" He said he sure did. "Then by the power IN-vested in me by the state of Oklahoma, I pronounce you husband and wife, partners in life, now and forever, and trust that you will take care of one another with love and kindness. Amen."

Jane squeezed me every time he said "trust" until I had to suppress giggles and finally whispered, "Stop it. I got it." It did seem like the old minister had been talking directly to me. I felt like I was getting to the place where I could trust Jane or, put another way, trust myself not to make another mistake when it came to love.

Wiley kissed the bride, we all gathered around to congratulate them, and then everyone broke for food, and dancing, and conversation. Wiley led Cal in a waltz, and he was a dapper little dancer, and I could see Cal was so proud to be showing him off.

I hugged Cal afterward. "You deserve the best, and it

looks like you finally got it," I said. She had tears in her eyes and flashed a big smile, and I knew she thought so too.

A good-sized fellow came up to Jane, and she introduced him to me as a friend of Sonny's who'd done a lot of work with her in her travels. He was jovial and imbibing. "Heard you two might be the next wedding," he said to me. "Now I need an invitation to that!" He winked at me, and I was embarrassed. "With the amount of people Jane knows, you'll need to rent an arena." Before Jane could answer, Mrs. Remington appeared—the conservative, no-undies, mother of Carolyne Remington. "Did I hear that you two are getting married? Now that's exciting," she said, and I was embarrassed again. I'd always pegged Mrs. No-underwear-Remington as a tight-ass, and here she was looking forward to a lesbian wedding. "We certainly are." Jane toasted her. Maybe I'd been too judgmental based on appearance. Not everyone who looked uptight was, it seemed. And Oklahomans, at least after a few glasses of wine, were far more liberal than even I knew. Then Mrs. Remington introduced us to the woman who was standing beside her, and I remembered seeing her occasionally at Carolyne's riding lessons.

"This is my partner, Abigail." I was stunned. Mrs. Remington was a lesbian, a single parent, and obviously the lesbian we were accused of favoring in her daughter's use of the arena.

"Well, you definitely get an invitation to the wedding now," I said, and we all laughed. As they walked away, I just stared. *Who knew? That is freaking amazing.*

Sonny joined us, looking especially pretty in cowgirl lace and leather, a big flower over her ear, and her long shiny black hair glistening in the sun. *Her dad must have had shiny black hair.* She slung her arm around me, in that same way Jane slung her arm over people. "You almost got me killed," she said, and I grinned. "That night at the hotel when I was teasing JB, and you thought I was some little hottie and you left, I thought JB was going to throw me over the balcony."

"Sorry," I said.

"It wasn't that bad," Jane said.

"Yes it was!" Sonny exclaimed. "She has a temper, but she doesn't explode. She just sort of percolates."

"Really? I've never seen that side of her." I lied, remembering Jane's steely expression when Steve Windom took his infamous flight off a pretend-bronc. Jane rolled her eyes before stepping away, maybe anticipating the private conversation Sonny was about to have with me.

Sonny was quiet for a moment. "JB's crazy about you. I've never seen her this way over anybody. So I hope you're the same about her, because I would never want to see her hurt." I noticed she called Jane JB and not Mom.

"Is this the speech that ends with 'because if you do hurt her, I'll kill you'?"

"Yep. This is that speech."

"I'm crazy about her. And I'm a stayer. I don't run off. But I've told her, I draw the line at infidelity, or anything that even remotely looks like it."

Sonny laughed. "She said you were tough."

"I am. But I will say, I need to slow down a bit and give the other person a moment to defend themselves before I blast off. I'm working on that."

"Okay then." She gave me a little toast. "You two might just be meant for each other." She headed off into the crowd to mingle.

A few moments later, Belle found me out by the shade tree, off the office porch, and brought me something to drink. I must have pulled back slightly, wary of any liquid proffered by a Windom, because she said, "There's nothing in it but Coke." That remark made me wonder if she knew what had happened.

I thanked her and said how happy Wiley looked, but she ignored that topic, having obviously planned this moment and had to get her say in.

"Ms. Starr, I'm begging you not to turn my mother in." She never mentioned her father, so I assumed she didn't know they worked as a pair.

"What are you talking about?" I stared at her. She was now a thinner fourteen-year-old. *She's the same age Jane was when Jane was pregnant.* It seemed almost impossible someone could rape a fourteen-year-old child.

"She told me," Belle said. "She said she came on to you when she was drunk, and you took offense, and now you're going to ruin our lives. Please don't hurt her."

I wanted to bust out of my own skin. That crazy Margaret had involved her daughter, lied to her, and made it appear I was some vindictive prude who wanted to get back at a drunk lady. I wanted to scream that her crazy, lying mother was a rapist and had drugged me, but what good would sharing that truth do? Before I could say anything, she wiped her eyes and walked away.

Jane, who always seemed to be keeping an eye out for me, casually strolled over.

"Sweet couple," she nodded toward the bride and groom. "What did Belle have to say?"

"Begged me not to hurt her mother, who told her she was drunk and came on to me, and I took offense. How horrific is it to include your kid in your fucked-up life? I don't know what to do."

"Same decision I had with Sonny. I didn't have the courage for an abortion, didn't really even know what that meant, and certainly no money or help in getting one. So I decided to keep the baby. Then I had to decide, would I send the baby's father to jail and later tell my daughter her dad was a jailbird rapist?"

"Are you sorry you didn't?"

"For myself, yes. For Sonny, no."

"So what does Sonny think happened with her biological father?"

"I told her the truth. He was her grandfather's best friend, and he helped me on the circuit after my dad, her grandfather, was killed bull riding. Then one night he raped me. I didn't report him because I was just a baby myself, and I didn't want her to have the legacy of a father who was in jail or registered for a sex crime."

"How'd she take that?"

"She just listened."

"Do you think he raped other women?"

"Truthfully, I don't know." She and I were both silent. "If he did," she finally said, "then it's my fault for not reporting him."

"If I bring charges against the Windoms, Belle's basically orphaned or living with relatives. If I don't bring charges, then does this thing just go on and on?"

"Or if you don't bring charges, does it just go on and on inside you?" Jane asked, and I didn't have an answer.

CHAPTER TWENTY-SIX

That evening, the newlyweds stopped by to hug us good-bye and tell us what a great wedding they'd had. Cal said, "You know, I don't know what's going to happen with Margaret-the-Molester, but I know you worry about Belle. You'd never admit it to anyone, but you do. Wiley and I talked about it, and if push came to shove, she could always room and board in the barn apartment over at the Barrow Ranch with us, I mean if she needed a place to go. And horses might keep her, if not sane, at least focused."

I figured Jane had planted that seed, and I told Cal that was a nice idea, and we'd just have to see how everything played out. Then there were more hugs, and they were off to the airport, headed for a honeymoon week at a resort in New Mexico that Jane had arranged through friends. I was still getting used to the fact that Jane had so many connections, when the only connection I cared about was the one she had with me.

❖

After a few days of picking up and cleaning up, Ellie and I had the ranch looking like nothing had ever taken place here.

Jane rode Dark Horse back and forth across the small divide between our ranches to talk, or have dinner, or make love, or just be together. At first, she stayed over occasionally, but after a few days, she spent every night at my ranch.

Today I had Lucky Lady saddled, and we rode our horses, side by side, out to the farthest end of the ranch. I still liked to watch Jane in the saddle even when she was just riding Dark Horse for pleasure. There was something so natural and yet erotic about the way she moved with the animal. We halted and sat there surveying the land and taking in the cool air. I felt whole.

"This is the most phenomenal horse," I said of my new mount. "She's so kind and loving and smooth under saddle. Where did you find her?"

"I looked for a while because I wanted her to be perfect for you—had to deliver on my promise to get you a new lover and a new horse."

"I love the horse. When's the new lover arriving?" I gave her a mischievous grin.

"Listen to you, torturing me like that."

"No lover but you, ever," I said.

"Better not be. Remember the fellow who loaned me Hedy Lemarr? Well, I bought Lucky Lady from him. He's a good trainer. And I've almost got him talked into selling me Hedy. I think Dark Horse would enjoy having a beautiful blonde stabled next to him on a cold winter's night." She leaned over and patted the famous gelding on his big neck. "The right horse is a perfect engagement gift for both of us. Next wedding's ours," she said. "We can get married right here in Oklahoma."

"You won't give up on that, will you?"

"Nope. Think we'll move into your place. Makes me feel like I'm sneaking around." I shot her a look. "That was payback, for 'when's the new lover arriving,'" she said, and I apologized, realizing Jane was more sensitive than she let on. "I'm never going out on you—because I love and adore you, and will never want anyone else."

"How can I know that?" I sighed, and she paused, I suppose to summon the right answer.

"Remember how in a cutting-horse competition, the rider finally drops her reins and commits the horse to the cow, and then there's no turning back? Well, I've committed. It's you."

"Are you calling me a cow?"

She laughed, "Well, I didn't mean it like that, but I do remember a woman calling me a grifter, and a womanizer, and God knows what all."

Ellie came riding up on one of the school horses, with the speed of the Pony Express. "It was on the news! Mrs. Windom's assistant has come forward and told police about Mrs. Windom's activities, and two unnamed victims have spoken to police about what she did to them." She was panting.

My cell phone rang immediately, and it was Jane's attorney asking if I'd heard the news. "Margaret Windom's attorneys have already been in touch. They're trying to put the lid on this thing as fast as possible, while at the same time saying they admit no wrongdoing, but they want to settle out of court."

"What made her assistant come forward?" I asked.

"Don't know. Maybe she saw what was going on and didn't want it to continue. Anyway, I'll be back in touch." The attorney hung up.

"Her assistant came forward," I repeated, amazed.

"Was she abused by her too?" Ellie asked in disgust, probably unable to forget my graphic account of that night and now believing every woman in Margaret's path was in danger.

"I doubt it. She was just a nice, matronly, Hispanic woman who was wearing a pretty cross around her neck. She seemed very kind."

"So this is good news, right?" Ellie beamed. "Now you're not alone."

"Right." I smiled at her, and she whirled her horse back around and took off like the town crier. And while I should have been upset, and worried and fearful about what was coming down in the press and on the news, I wasn't any longer. Truth was truth.

"I don't think I ever thanked you for having your attorney call me," I said quietly to Jane, and she signaled Dark Horse to move sideways, adjacent to Lucky Lady, leaned over, and kissed me.

"You're welcome."

"I don't think I've ever been kissed on horseback before," I said. "And come to think of it, you're a little too smooth at it, like you've done it before."

She just laughed at me, and we rode on, happy to be together. I felt, for the first time, that I wouldn't have to face things alone.

A rumble of thunder and streaks of lightning in the distance warned us to take the horses back to the barn, where we unsaddled them and turned them loose in the pasture. They rolled in the dirt to let us know they wanted all human smells off them. I laughed at their antics and walked arm in arm with Jane up to the house. "So now we have two big houses," I said, "and we don't need that."

"I was thinking of putting Cal and Wiley in my place," she said. "And me moving over here with you." I must have looked nervous, because she laughed. "Uh-huh. Be careful what you wish for. You'd have me twenty-four-seven, and come to think

of it, I don't know if I could take that much bossing around."
We were indoors and headed for the bedroom. "Plus, I have a
lot of wardrobe." She peered into the closet.

"I know. A hat and shirt and boots for every day of the
year," I said.

"It's all part of the mystique."

"I noticed. Like the sexy way you get out of your SUV,
slooowly close the door, tilt the sunglasses."

She moved in close to me and put her arms around me.
"All calculated moves designed to attract the right woman,
and I would say they worked." She kissed me. We chucked our
clothes and got into the shower together. She soaped me down
as I continued my inquisition.

"Seriously, what would you do if another woman said she
wanted you?" I asked.

"I'd say I'm flattered, but I am with my true love." Her
tone was slow and sultry, and she was turning our showering
into an erotic play-date, so I wrestled with her a little to try to
get her to let up, until I could get answers to my question.

"I'm asking because I have to trust you," I said, trying to
ignore that she was soaping me down and rubbing my entire
body.

"Now trust is like riding a spirited horse." She stroked me
gently, running her fingers inside me, then playfully sliding
them out, making it impossible for me to concentrate. "The
horse can hurt you, it's true, but if you trust her…" She was
making me delirious with her lovemaking and simultaneous
conversation. "The horse tends to sense that you trust her, and
she wants to live up to that." She was in me, full on, and I was
out of my mind as she held me up against her and I climaxed.

"All except stallions. They just fuck everything in sight,"
she murmured.

"You'd better not be a stallion," I said, grabbing her anatomy, and she yelped.

"Think of me as a gelding." Jane chuckled, referencing a castrated stallion. "That's a stallion with memories." I punched her playfully and insisted we get out of the shower because I could hear rain beating down on the roof, a sign that lightning might be next.

We hopped into bed, still damp, but not as wet on the outside as we were in. She reached over the side of the bed, and picked up something, and handed it to me.

"What is this?" I held up the gold and diamonds with the light bouncing off them.

"It's called an engagement ring," she teased. "When the tree's alive, you've got to break out the ornaments." And she slid the ring on my finger. It was gorgeous, and I was astounded.

"It's absolutely the most beautiful piece of jewelry I've ever owned, from the most beautiful woman I've ever known. It fits perfectly. How did you know my ring size?"

"I've had some experience with those fingers," she said. "Are you going to marry me, Rae Starr?"

"I can see you're a woman who has to button everything up," I teased her back softly, and then became serious. "I am definitely going to marry you, Jane Barrow." And I kissed her, like I'd never kissed anyone in my life. "Will we always make mad, passionate love—even when I'm sixty-eight and you're eighty?" I asked.

"Of course, if you stay in shape so you can keep up." She gave me the Barrow grin. And I laughed, because I was sure that would be the case.

A loud, startling sound of thunder rumbled overhead like a herd of horses running across the prairie. Lightning crashed, lighting up the sky, and heavy rain suddenly pelted the bedroom windows. I felt inexplicably safe and happy and loved, lying in her arms. The storm had finally moved in…and she was mine.

About the Authors

Andrews & Austin began their writing careers in Los Angeles developing and optioning theatricals and movies-of-the-week. They spent decades in the entertainment field, Andrews as a writer/producer and studio executive, Austin as a television producer and on-air talent. Both have ranching backgrounds. Andrews was raised on her grandmother's horse ranch in Oklahoma, while Austin spent time on her aunt's cattle ranch in New Mexico. Andrews & Austin now live on their own ranch on the prairie with Icelandic horses and an assortment of dogs and cats. They can be contacted at AndrewsAustin@gmail.com.

Books Available From Bold Strokes Books

Bet Against Me by Fiona Riley. In the high-stakes luxury real estate market, everything has a price, and as rival Realtors Trina Lee and Kendall Yates find out, that means their hearts and souls, too. (978-1-63555-729-9)

Broken Reign by Sam Ledel. Together on an epic journey in search of a mysterious cure, a princess and a village outcast must overcome life-threatening challenges and their own prejudice if they want to survive. (978-1-63555-739-8)

Just One Taste by CJ Birch. For Lauren, it only took one taste to start trusting in love again. (978-1-63555-772-5)

Lady of Stone by Barbara Ann Wright. Sparks fly as a magical emergency forces a noble embarrassed by her ability to submit to a low-born teacher who resents everything about her. (978-1-63555-607-0)

Last Resort by Angie Williams. Katie and Rhys are about to find out what happens when you meet the girl of your dreams but you aren't looking for a happily ever after. (978-1-63555-774-9)

Longing for You by Jenny Frame. When Debrek housekeeper Katie Brekman is attacked amid a burgeoning vampire-witch war, Alexis Villiers must go against everything her clan believes in to save her. (978-1-63555-658-2)

Money Creek by Anne Laughlin. Clare Lehane is a troubled lawyer from Chicago who tries to make her way in a rural town full of secrets and deceptions. (978-1-63555-795-4)

Passion's Sweet Surrender by Ronica Black. Cam and Blake are unable to deny their passion for each other, but surrendering to love is a whole different matter. (978-1-63555-703-9)

The Holiday Detour by Jane Kolven. It will take everything going wrong to make Dana and Charlie see how right they are for each other. (978-1-63555-720-6)

Too Hot to Ride by Andrews & Austin. World-famous cutting horse champion and industry legend Jane Barrow is knockdown sexy in the way she moves, talks, and rides, and Rae Starr is determined not to get involved with this womanizing gambler. (978-1-63555-776-3)

A Love that Leads to Home by Ronica Black. For Carla Sims and Janice Carpenter, home isn't about location, it's where your heart is. (978-1-63555-675-9)

Blades of Bluegrass by D. Jackson Leigh. A US Army occupational therapist must rehab a bitter veteran who is a ticking political time bomb the military is desperate to disarm. (978-1-63555-637-7)

Hopeless Romantic by Georgia Beers. Can a jaded wedding planner and an optimistic divorce attorney possibly find a future together? (978-1-63555-650-6)

Hopes and Dreams by PJ Trebelhorn. Movie theater manager Riley Warren is forced to face her high school crush and tormentor, wealthy socialite Victoria Thayer, at their twentieth reunion. (978-1-63555-670-4)

In the Cards by Kimberly Cooper Griffin. Daria and Phaedra are about to discover that love finds a way, especially when powers outside their control are at play. (978-1-63555-717-6)

Moon Fever by Ileandra Young. SPEAR agent Danika Karson must clear her werewolf friend of multiple false charges while teaching her vampire girlfriend to resist the blood mania brought on by a full moon. (978-1-63555-603-2)

Serenity by Jesse J. Thoma. For Kit Marsden, there are many things in life she cannot change. Serenity is in the acceptance. (978-1-63555-713-8)

Sylver and Gold by Michelle Larkin. Working feverishly to find a killer before he strikes again, Boston homicide detective Reid Sylver and rookie cop London Gold are blindsided by their chemistry and developing attraction. (978-1-63555-611-7)